A BOOK OF
CHARMS
AND
CHANGELINGS

A BOOK OF

CHARMS
AND
CHANGELINGS

Ruth Manning-Sanders

illustrated by Robin Jacques

E. P. DUTTON & CO., INC.   NEW YORK

First published in the U.S.A. 1972 by E. P. Dutton
Copyright © 1971 by Ruth Manning-Sanders

SBN: 0-525-26775-1   LCC: 71-179053
Printed in the U.S.A.
First Edition

Contents

Foreword

A Changeling, so the dictionaries tell us, is a person (usually a child) stealthily put in place of another. And so we find many stories about fairies snatching babies from their cradles, and leaving some tiresome little creature of their own in the baby's place. Why do the fairies do this? It seems for no reason, except pure love of mischief. Anyway, there is the poor mother left with an ugly little goblin to feed and tend, and having all the trouble in the world to get her own baby back again. She tries all sorts of ways: one way is to leave the changeling in the churchyard till midnight, as Janey does in the Cornish stroy, *Tredrill.* Another way is to threaten to toss the thing into the fire, as in the Finnish story, *The Flute Player.*

But in this book you will also find changelings other than babies. There is the soldier changeling in *The Hat,* a story which comes from Esthonia; there is the raven changeling in the North American Indian story, *The Ogre, the Sun, and the Raven;* and there is the girl changeling in the Chinese story, *Chien-Nang* – surely the most mysterious changeling that ever existed!

As for *Charms* – those spells that work magic for good or for ill – all fairy stories are full of them. Generally the charms are worked by amulets: little objects that protect from evil, or bring good fortune, and which the lucky possessor of them must wear round his or her neck, or carry in a pocket, or keep in some safe place; for woe betide the one who, possessing such an amulet, should happen to lose it!

Such amulets you will find in the Bosnian story, *The Magic*

7

Bridle (the bridle itself); in the Korean story, *The Enchanted Wine Jug* (a piece of amber); and in *Pancakes and Pies*, a story that comes from Russia, in which the little sky-blue handmill with the golden handle is the amulet that grinds out food for the hungry old man and woman.

Then there is the cap that makes the wearer invisible, in *The Dwarf with the Long Beard*, a story told by the Slav peasants and herdsmen; and also in this story there is the Dwarf's beard itself, the amulet which awakens the princess from her deadly sleep. In the Gypsy tale of *Fedor and the Fairy* the amulets are three whistles, given to Fedor by the Kings of the Wind, the Moon and the Sun. In the Sicilian story, *Peppi*, the charm is contained in the bones of the old ox, which transform a piece of bare ground into a fragrant orchard. In *The White Lamb*, a story from Brittany, there is the little golden wand, given to Rosalie by her fairy godmother; the amulet which protects Rosalie from the beatings of her cruel step-mother. But alas for Rosalie when she loses that golden wand! Then comes the witch, brewing evil charms in her cauldron, and turning poor Rosalie into a white lamb. For there are bad charms as well as good ones, and these bad charms are not worked by amulets. Some are worked by the brewing of poisonous herbs, some by the muttered spells of a sorcerer, as in *The Forty Goats*, a story from the Valley of the Nile.

There are also powerful beings who can charm one thing into another by their mere will. The Storm King, for instance, in the Transylvanian story of *The Sun Mother*, can in an instant transform himself into a grey horse. And then there is the mountain demon *Rubizal*, in the story from Silesia – and what cannot Rubizal do? By his charms he can produce a magnificent tavern in the heart of the lonely mountains; he can change the tavern servants into all sorts of grotesque shapes; he can make the pictured tapestries on the walls of the tavern come alive; he can make the ceiling of that tavern pour down torrents of rain; and he can wreck the whole place in a mad storm of thunder and lightening. Nor is that all; the insolent lord of the manor and his companions he can transform into pigs and weasels, asses and toads. And all this havoc he can work without saying a word!

No, it doesn't do to insult such powerful beings. And so we are warned. We must behave ourselves. We must do good and not ill. If we remember this simple maxim we are safe. Then let witches and wizards do their worst: all the charms of the fairy world will eventually work together to protect us.

1 · The Magic Bridle

There was a lad who lived with his stepmother, and she was always scolding. It seemed he could do nothing to please her. So one day he took his gun and walked off into the mountains. Should he now try to shoot some game to carry home to his stepmother, or should he now shoot himself, and be done with her scoldings for ever?

Well, there he was, all in the dumps, when he looked down and saw a great lake. And in the lake was a creature the like of which he'd never seen before. Sometimes it seemed to be a stag, and then again it seemed to be a horse; and it was diving down and coming up, and diving down again, and it was green all over. And it came out of the water and frolicked on the shore, and still the lad couldn't tell what manner of creature it was. But whatever it was, it was green as grass, and it was wearing a bridle. Well then, if it's wearing a bridle, it must be a horse . . . but then it's got horns!

'Don't care what you are,' mutters the lad, 'I'll shoot you!' So – *bang*!

Well now, plague take it, he's missed! The creature's gone back into the lake and disappeared. But it's left the bridle on the shore.

The lad runs down to pick up the bridle. And the creature puts its horned head out of the water and laughs at him. *Ha! ha! ha! Ha! ha! ha!* So the lad thinks to pitch the bridle after the creature, but the creature calls out, 'Don't do that! The bridle's a present for you, and a precious one. It can turn anything into anything. It can turn a pig into a princess, or a prince into a frog. You have only to strike anything with it and say, "Be this! Be that!" and it *will* be this or that. Ha! Ha! Who's got the whip hand now – you or that shrew of a stepmother?'

So the lad took the bridle and set off home again.

And on the way home he met a cow. He struck the cow with the bridle and said, 'Be a very beautiful horse.' And the cow changed herself into a horse, the finest in all the world. The lad took the horse to market, and sold it for a handful of gold. So off with him home, merry as a lark, thinking his stepmother will surely be pleased with him this time!

Was she pleased? Well, she grinned a bit when he gave her the money, but she was soon scowling again and wanting to know how he'd come by it. And when he told her, she said he must have sold himself to the devil, and she howled till the platters on the shelf rang. And then she snatches the bridle from him, gives him a whack with it, and screams out, 'You base knave, be a dog!'

And there he is, a lad no longer, but a great shaggy sheep dog. And she takes a broom and chases him out of the house.

Away runs that great shaggy sheep dog, away and away, and comes to the shepherd who tends the emperor's sheep. 'Ho, ho! my fine fellow,' says the shepherd, 'will you work for me?'

And the great shaggy sheep dog wags his tail. So now he's guarding the emperor's sheep, and he guards them well. Should a thief think to steal, should a wolf think to kill one of those sheep – let him beware! Our great shaggy sheep dog is on him in an instant. The wolf is throttled, and the thief is brought to the emperor, howling for mercy.

Now the emperor was an unhappy man, because every time his wife had a baby, a witch came from the mountains and carried it off. This had happened six times; and when a seventh child was born, a beautiful baby boy, the emperor felt desperate. How to protect his little son from a thief who came no one knew how, and went without being seen?

Then the emperor's shepherd said, 'Your majesty, put my sheep dog to guard the cradle. He can smell things that we cannot, and he can hear sounds that we cannot; and I promise you he will be faithful to the death.'

So the great shaggy sheep dog was brought to the palace, and lay at night beside the baby's cradle. With his head on his paws, and his ears cocked, he watched and listened.

At the door of the baby's nursery the emperor had posted a guard of armed soldiers; and in the nursery itself, besides the great shaggy sheep dog, there were six nurses and thirty pages. And all these people had been warned not to fall asleep on peril of their lives. But what would you? In the dead of night the witch came: she waved her wand and whispered 'Let all the people in the palace fall into a deep sleep and not waken until dawn!' So the emperor fell asleep, and the empress fell asleep, and the watchmen at the baby's door fell asleep. And the witch passed by the sleeping watchmen at the baby's door, and went into the baby's room, where the nurses and the pages lay sprawled and snoring. . . .

But the great shaggy sheep dog was wide, wide awake – ah ha! When the witch said '*people*' she hadn't said '*animals*'! And as she stoops, thinking to lift the baby from the cradle – one jump and that great shaggy sheep dog has her by the throat. *Gr-gr-gr-gr!* How he shakes her, how he worries her! And in the morning, when the emperor wakes – what does he see standing by his bed? The great shaggy sheep dog wagging his tail, and carrying in his mouth something that looks like a bundle of twigs bound round with rag. What is it? The skinny body of the dead witch.

The emperor sent his soldiers up into the mountains to the dead witch's house; and there they found the emperor's other six children. The witch had turned them into mice, but as soon as she was dead they took their proper shape again. And the soldiers brought them back to the palace. So the emperor was as happy now as he had before been miserable. And in his gratitude he gave our shaggy sheep dog a fine gold medal to hang round his neck.

Then the shaggy sheep dog runs home to the stepmother and says, 'Stepmother, I have brought you a fine gold medal. I beg you in return to strike me with the bridle, that I may become a man again.'

The stepmother snatches the gold medal, she strikes the great shaggy sheep dog: but, oh, the wretch – what is she saying?

'*You* giving yourself airs! Be an ugly little mongrel that nobody wants – and get out of here!'

And there he is, a poor ugly little mongrel, crouched at her feet; and she takes the broom and chases him out of the house.

The poor ugly little mongrel whom nobody wanted, wandered here, wandered there, glad enough to find an old bone in an ash heap, or a crust in the gutter. And being soon half dead with hunger, he went again to the stepmother. 'I beseech you to strike me with the bridle that I may become a man again, for otherwise I shall surely die!'

'Oh ho! Who talks of dying?' says she. And she gives him a blow with the bridle and says, 'Be a wren and seek your food in the forest!' And the ugly little mongrel turned into a wren and flew away into the forest.

Now life was not too bad for the little wren. He picked up insects and spiders to eat, and sang his little songs, and felt happy for a while. But then winter came, snow fell, the little wren was cold, and thought longingly of the glowing fire in the stepmother's kitchen. And one dark evening he fluttered out of the forest, and came back to the stepmother's house.

The stepmother was dozing by the fire, and the bridle was hanging on a peg behind the door. The wren flew up, pecked the bridle with his little beak and made it swing. The bridle hit the little wren on the head, and the little wren cried out, 'Let the wren be a man!' And there was the lad standing by the hearth with the bridle in his hand.

Then he gave the stepmother a tap with the bridle and said, 'Be an owl and do your screeching in the woods, if screech you must!' And the stepmother turned into an owl, and the lad opened the window and she flew out.

So after that the lad lived in peace. And he lived in plenty too. Well, how shouldn't he? If the cupboard was bare he had only to strike it with the bridle and say, 'Be full of food!' And if his purse was empty he had but to strike it with the bridle and say, 'Be full of money!' And so it was with everything he needed.

But the best thing that ever he did in his life has yet to be told. One day he met a pretty smiling girl, and showed her the bridle. And whilst she bent to look at it, he gently tapped her with it on the head and said, 'Be my sweet and loving wife, and may we never quarrel!'

And that's what happened.

2 · Chien-Nang

Long ago in China there lived a rich, busy man called Chang, who had a beautiful daughter, called Chien-Nang. He also had a nephew called Wang-Chou, and this nephew came to work for Chang, to do his accounts and suchlike. Well now, what had to happen, did happen. Chien-Nang, the beautiful daughter, and Wang-Chou, the nephew, fell in love. Ah, how dearly they loved each other!

But old Chang had other ideas for his daughter. He betrothed her to a rich friend of his; and he told Wang-Chou, quite kindly, that he had better go away and earn his living somewhere else.

'You see, my dear nephew,' said Chang, 'it won't do. Chien-Nang must marry according to her rank, and you are but a poor scholar.' Then he gave Wang-Chou some money and plenty of food, and put him in a little boat to sail down the river to Nanking.

And when Chien-Nang saw Wang-Chou go, she said, 'My heart is broken.' And she lay down on her bed and wept.

Wang-Chou sailed away down the river, and at sunset he drew the boat into shore that he might eat and sleep. But he couldn't eat, he couldn't sleep. He lay awake till midnight, thinking of his dear love, Chien-Nang.

And at midnight, as he lay awake, looking up at the stars and sorrowing – what did he hear? Footsteps, little light footsteps running along the bank of the river. And next moment – there was Chien-Nang leaping barefoot into the boat.

'I must come with you! I *will* come with you!' cried she. 'I love no one but you; I will wed no one but you!'

So Wang-Chou, laughing with joy, wrapped her in a blanket and snuggled her down in the bottom of the boat, where none might see her. He pushed the boat from shore and away they sailed, away and away, night and day, night and day, till they came to the city of Nanking. And there they were married.

Wang-Chou got work as a scribe; he didn't earn much, but he earned enough to keep them from want. And so five years passed. But Chien-Nang was restless. 'My dear husband,' said she, 'I keep thinking and thinking of my father. I hope he has forgiven us; but how can I be sure? I want to go home, I want to fall at my father's feet, I want him to lift me up, I want to hear him say, "All is forgiven, my little daughter." Then truly we three can rejoice together.'

And Wang-Chou said, 'If that is your wish, dear wife, let us go.'

So they took a boat and sailed away up the river to return to the father's house.

And when they came to the shore under Chang's house, Wang-Chou said, 'Wife, stay you here in the boat, I will go alone up to the house. It may be that your father is still very angry; and it is I who must bear the blame and try to make the peace. If he has forgiven us, then I will return and bring you to him.'

So Chien-Nang stayed in the boat, and Wang-Chou walked up to Chang's house; and there was Chang sitting in the garden. Wang-Chou thought to bow down before him, but Chang leaped up and took Wang-Chou in his arms. 'My dear, dear nephew,' cried he, 'I am rejoiced to see you! How has it fared with you all these years?'

'It has fared with us very well, my uncle,' said Wang-Chou. 'Very well with both me and my wife.'

'Your wife – then you are married, Wang-Chou?'

'Oh yes, my uncle, we married as soon as we got to Nanking. And if you have forgiven us, Chien-Nang is waiting in the boat, and I will fetch her.'

18

'But – but – but –' cried Chang, staring and stammering. 'What is this you are saying, nephew? Chien-Nang lies on her bed, sick and nigh to death! She fell ill of grief the very hour that you left us. Ah, how bitterly have I repented the hour that I sent you away! Never since then has my darling daughter lifted up her head or smiled. The doctors can do nothing for her – they say she will die of a broken heart.'

'Oh me!' thought Wang-Chou. 'My uncle has gone out of his mind! The shock of losing Chien-Nang has turned his brain!' And he spoke gently as if to an invalid. 'Dear uncle,' said he, 'Chien-Nang is not ill; she is waiting in the boat for me to bring her to you.'

Then Chang looked sorrowfully at his nephew. 'Poor lad, poor lad,' thought he, 'I did very wrong to drive him away. Ah, how those two young people must have loved one another! Now, through grieving, my darling daughter lies on her death-bed; and, through grieving, my dear nephew has lost his wits. And it is all my fault!'

So Chang spoke gently to Wang-Chou, as if to an invalid.

'Nephew,' said he, 'whomsoever you married, it was not my daughter. And whoever is in the boat it is not Chien-Nang. For, as I have told you, Chien-Nang has lain on her sick-bed these five long years. See now, I will order my servants to carry her down here into the garden – for seeing is believing, dear nephew.'

'Yes, seeing is believing, uncle!' cried Wang-Chou. 'I assure you that Chien-Nang is well and longing to see you. She is waiting in the boat to come to you. I will run and fetch her!'

So Wang-Chou ran off to the boat to fetch his wife. And Chang called his servants and ordered them to carry his daughter out into the garden. But when the servants went into Chien-Nang's room – what did they see? No lovesick dying maiden lying on the bed, but a maiden up and dressed, blooming with health, laughing, lovely.

And laughing, lovely Chien-Nang runs out into the garden: runs out to meet – whom? Another Chien-Nang, laughing, lovely, coming up from the boat. . . .

Laughing, lovely, the two Chien-Nangs spring into each other's arms: like two bright water drops they melt one into the other. And lo – where there were two Chien-Nangs, there is now only one.

Which was the real Chien-Nang, and which the changeling? The wise men of China argued about that for a long, long time. But let them argue as they would, they could not decide. And if Chien-Nang herself knew, she never told them.

3 · The Enchanted Wine Jug

Once upon a time there was an old man who lived on the banks of a big broad river. There was a high road on one side of the river, and a high road on the other side; and ferry boats went to and fro, to and fro, ferrying travellers and their carriages and their horses across from one high road to the other.

Now our old man's little house stood on the north side of the river, close to the quay where the ferry boats came to shore; and so he was able to earn a copper or two making taut a rope to a bollard, or steadying a gangway, or hastening to the head of a frightened horse as it came stamping off the ferry boat on to the quay.

Well, of course he didn't earn much; but he was a contented old man, and though he had no near neighbours, he didn't feel lonely. He had a cat and a dog for company. He chatted away to his cat and dog by the hour, and they chatted away to him; they had a language that all three of them could understand.

Now one scorching hot day, after the ferry boat had come and gone, and all the passengers had driven or ridden or walked away to refresh themselves at an inn in the nearest village, the old man went into his little house and sat him down to refresh himself also. He was hot, he was tired, he was very, very thirsty. He had set his wine jug and a chipped cup on the table, and was just about to pour himself out a cup of wine, when there came a knock at the door.

The old man sighed, got up, went to the door and opened it.

And there stood a young fellow dressed in rags and covered with dust.

'Of your charity a drop of wine,' gasped the young fellow, 'for my tongue cleaves to the roof of my mouth with thirst!'

'Ah well, guests first is only manners,' thought our old man. And he handed the wine jug and the cup to the stranger. 'Help thyself!' said he.

The stranger didn't bother to fill the cup. He set the wine jug to his lips, tilted back his head and drank, drank, drank. How he drank! Our old man was first amused, and then worried. 'If the young fellow goes on that way he'll empty the jug,' thought he. 'And then what am *I* to drink?'

'Isn't your thirst quenched yet?' he asked.

The stranger shook his head. He went on drinking, drinking, drinking. And when he set down the jug, that jug was empty.

'I thank you greatly,' said he to the old man. 'And now I will repay you.' And he took a little piece of amber from a wallet at his girdle, and dropped it into the empty jug. 'So long as this charm stays in your jug, your jug will always be full,' said he. And then – well, what do you think? – he vanished. First he was there, and then he was gone, and left our old man with his eyes nigh popping out of his head, and staring at nothing.

'Did you ever?' says he to his cat and his dog. 'That must have been a fairy man, surely. And a fairy man is something you don't see every day, my children.'

But what about the wine jug? Yes, it was full to the brim. And when the old man poured out some of the wine into his cup, that wine sparkled like rubies in sunlight. And when he put the cup to his lips and took a draught of that wine – ah, what wine! Never, never in his life had the old man tasted anything so delicious, so thirst-quenching, so heartening, so strength-giving, so pure, so – No, there were no words to describe the flavour of that wine. Both food and drink it seemed to be, food and drink and the assurance that all was well. The dog must have a taste, the cat must have a taste! 'If the wine in this jug never grows less, we're in luck's way, my darlings,' said the old man. And both the cat and the dog agreed with him.

That night, when the old man had gone to bed, the dog and the cat sat up talking. They had a bright idea. But into which of their heads that bright idea first jumped, I can't tell you. Anyway, early in the morning they woke the old man with their clamouring, both trying to talk at once and each one interrupting the other.

'Master,' says the dog, 'you are poor, very poor.'

'That's true enough,' chuckled the old man.

'Master,' says the cat, 'you have now a wine jug that never grows empty.'

'Seems that's true enough also,' laughs the old man.

'Then, master,' shouted the dog, 'why not open a little shop. . . .'

'And sell your wine in pennyworths, and two pennyworths, and sixpennyworths to the folk who come and go by ferry?' cries the cat.

'I might do worse,' says the old man.

'You couldn't do better!' shouted both the cat and the dog together.

So our old man opened his little wine shop, and sure enough he prospered. The fame of the wine he had to offer spread through all the countryside, and the pennies and the twopennies and the sixpennies poured into the old man's pocket. Everyone landing from the ferry boats, or waiting to cross the river, must drink a cup of that old man's wine. And whatever might be their troubles before they drank, as soon as they had drained their cup all their troubles seemed to have vanished.

People came, too, from all the country round, bringing their empty jugs and bottles to be filled.

'Hey, old man, give us some of your good wine to carry home, that our days may be bright, and our sleep calm and happy!'

The old man grew rich; he and the cat and the dog lived in clover. The dog had a silver collar, the cat had a gold ball to play with, the old man bought himself a handsome suit of clothes, and a chest to keep his spare money in.

But what puzzled everybody was where the old man kept all the wine he sold. He seemed to have no store of barrels in his little house. Always when a customer came, he would pour out wine from the same old jug, trot into some back place with the empty jug, and come trotting in again with the jug as full as ever. Well, good luck to him anyway, his customers said. An old fellow who could produce wine that made everyone feel good and happy, deserved to have his little secrets!

But alas, alas, there came a day when the old man, having emptied the wine jug in serving some customers, trotted out as usual into the back place in the pretence of refilling it. And he was just about to trot back again to serve more customers, when it struck him that the jug felt astonishingly light. What had happened? He peered into the jug: no joyous sparkle of ruby fluid met his eye. He tipped the jug sideways, shook it, put his ear to it. He heard no joyous slosh-slosh of liquid. He turned the jug upside down. Yes, it was empty, there was nothing in it, nothing! And the little piece of amber was gone from inside it.

The old man hurried to his customers. 'I'm sorry, gentlemen, I've run out of wine. Perhaps if you would come again tomorrow?'

Oh yes, they would all come again tomorrow – he might be sure of that! And away they went, carrying their empty jugs and bottles, disappointed, but hoping for better luck next day.

The old man called his cat and his dog. 'The jug is empty, my darlings. The amber's fallen out, seemingly. But the amber must be somewhere about the house, and we must find it before tomorrow.'

So they began to search the house: the dog sniffing along the floor, the cat climbing up on to chairs and tables, the old man peering into cupboards, and shifting the crockery on the shelves.

But not a blink of that amber did any of them see. And as the day passed, and it was night, and the night too was passing, their search became quite frantic. Dragging the furniture about, poking in the ashes of the fire, scattering plates and dishes, toppling the bread out of the bin, tumbling the blankets from the old man's bed, overturning the cat's basket, pulling at the dog's rug, they ran up and down shouting at one another. The dog was growling, the cat was spitting, the old man was shedding tears: they were quarrelling for the first time in their lives; and by dawn the little house was a shambles. But still they hadn't found that piece of amber.

What to do? Oh, what to do? There was nothing for it but to lock the door, pull down the blinds and nail up a notice outside: NO WINE TODAY.

And when they had done that, and begged each other's pardon for quarrelling, they lay down and slept, for they were worn out, all three of them.

NO WINE TODAY, the notice said. But today became to-morrow, and tomorrow became next day, and though they searched and searched, they couldn't find the amber.

No wine today, no wine tomorrow, no more wine on any tomorrow! No more pennies, or twopennies or sixpennies coming in, and the days passing, and the weeks, and the months. The old man taking his saved-up money from the chest to buy food and fuel: a little today, a little tomorrow. . . . But many littles make a much, and the money was going, was going, was going! The old man took off his fine suit of clothes and laid it away in the empty chest, together with the dog's silver collar, and the cat's gold ball. No, he couldn't bear to sell those things! But all the same there came a day when he had to take them out of the chest and sell them. And it wasn't long before he was as poor as he had ever been, and hovering on the river bank again to pick up a copper or two by helping the ferry men or the passengers.

And in the evenings the old man and the cat and the dog could talk about nothing but that little piece of amber. The old man thought the fairy man must have called it back. But the cat and the dog wouldn't agree to that – it would be too mean a trick!

'Perhaps I vexed the fairy man,' said the old man meekly.

'*You*, master!' said the cat. 'You never vexed anyone in all your life!'

'But if the fairy hasn't taken it back and it's not in the house, said the old man, 'where is it?'

'Why, somewhere *outside* the house, to be sure,' said the dog.

And then the cat gave a shriek. 'I have it! I have it! You poured it out with the last of the wine into somebody's jug, and that somebody walked away with it all unknowingly!'

Yes, they agreed that was what must have happened. But who was that somebody, and where could they find him?

So then the cat and the dog decided to go out each day and search through every street and every house in the neighbouring villages, and in every lonely farmhouse or solitary cottage. The cat said she was sure her whiskers would bristle if she came near that piece of amber; and the dog said he was sure his nose would smell it out, if *he* came anywhere near it. So off they set. The cat ran along the roof tops, peering and prying, jumping in through windows, crawling under furniture, climbing up on to shelves, and crouching outside cupboards, waiting for her whiskers to bristle; but they never did. The dog ran along the streets, and in and out of farmyards and cottage gardens, busily sniffing. But though a thousand thousand scents, both pleasant and unpleasant, came drifting into his enquiring nostrils, the smell of that little piece of amber was not amongst them.

It seemed that all the reward they got from their busy seeking was an occasional whack with a stick, or smack from a stone at the hands of some indignant householder. So that sometimes the dog limped home covered with bruises, and the cat crept back with a bleeding cheek or paw. And then the old man would cry over them, and say they must give up the search. But no, they wouldn't.

Now it was spring, then it was summer, and then it was autumn – they were still searching, whilst the old man hovered about the ferry boats to earn the few pennies that kept the three of them from starving. And then came the cold, cold winter, and the water in the river froze solid from bank to bank. No more ferry boats: the travellers were now crossing from bank to bank in their carriages, or astride their horses; and the pedlars and pilgrims were shuffling over the ice in snowshoes. No more pennies now to be earned by our old man: wrapped in a blanket and blue with cold, he must hover on the river bank and trust to charity.

'Brother,' said the cat to the dog, 'we have searched in every place, likely and unlikely, on this side of the river – but what about that town on the opposite bank?'

'Sister,' said the dog, 'let us go and search there!'

So they raced across the frozen river and came to the town and began their diligent searching. They searched every night, but by day they raced back across the ice to the old man, lest he mope for lack of their company. But they were no more successful in their search on the far side of the river, than they had been on the near side.

'Give up, give up, my darlings,' said the old man. 'It's hopeless!'

But the cat glared, and the dog growled. They would not give up, they would *not*!

And then, with the coming of spring, the ice began to break. The river was aswirl with floating ice blocks and rushing water. And one morning the cat and dog, after their night's search, found there was no crossing the river to get home again. Then indeed the old man mourned. 'I have lost my amber and I have lost my wealth, and that is bad enough,' he wept. 'But now I have lost my two darling children, and that is worst of all!'

But that very night the dog said, 'Cat, we have searched all through this town, and we have found nothing. But there is a village over yonder where we have not yet searched. Let us go there.'

'Yes,' said the cat, 'let us go there.'

And they went to the village. The dog ran sniff, sniff, sniffing through the village street, the cat went prowling over the roof tops. And at the very last roof she came to – what was this? Her whiskers bristled! Then the amber was in that house! It must be! It must be! The cat nearly fell off the roof in her excitement. She did a dance all by herself in the moonlight. Then she pulled herself together and scrambled down a chimney. Where was she now? In an attic bedroom where a man lay asleep and snoring peacefully.

Creeping noiselessly here, creeping noiselessly there, guided by the greater or lesser bristling of her whiskers, the cat jumped on to the top of a high clothes press. And on the top of that clothes press lay an old tobacco box of dusty soapstone. If the cat's whiskers had been bristling before, they bristled now so fiercely that they stuck out like needles. The amber they had been searching for all these months was in that box – the cat felt sure of it!

And she was right. Long ago the man, who now lay sleeping on his bed, had gone one day to the old man's shop, carrying an empty jar. He had got his jar filled, paid his sixpence, returned home across the ferry, and up in his little attic bedroom had made merry with some friends of his over such wine as they had none of them thought to exist on earth. And in pouring the last wine out of his jar, he had also poured out a little piece of amber. . . . A little piece of amber – what use is that to him? Well, maybe he might one day find a use for it. So in the meantime he had stowed it away in an empty tobacco box on the top of his clothes press, and by and by had forgotten all about it.

Now the cat, trembling with excitement, tried to carry the box away in her mouth. But it was too big and too heavy for that little mouth. She tried to bite open the lid of the box, but the soapstone was too hard for her little teeth. What to do? She scrambled up the chimney again and ran to take counsel with the dog.

'We must find the king of the rats,' said the dog. 'And we must find him quickly.'

So they ran here, and they ran there, looking for the king of the the rats; but it was not till morning that they found him. He was sitting before a scrap of looking glass down in a cellar. He was wearing a little crown of coloured paper, and having his coat combed and brushed by two attendants, for he was a very vain old fellow.

'What do you mean by coming here disturbing majesty at his toilet?' he snapped at the cat and the dog. 'And what do you want?'

Well, what they wanted was that some of his people should gnaw the soapstone box open, and get out the amber. But the king of the rats was on his dignity. Why should any of his people risk damaging their teeth in such a trumpery cause?

So then the cat and the dog promised that if he would only do what they asked, they would make a ten years' truce with his majesty. And during that time they would neither of them chase or trouble or even snap at one of his subjects. If they so much as set eyes on a rat during those ten years, they promised to turn their heads aside, and look another way.

'Very well,' said his majesty. And he gave three shrill squeaks. And at each squeak rats and more rats came scampering out of their holes in the cellar.

Then the king of the rats told them what they must do; and as soon as the man who lived in the attic had gone to work, a whole army of rats raced to the attic, swarmed up on to the top of the clothes press, and took it in turns to gnaw at the lid of the soap-stone box. The soapstone was not hard, as stones go, but still it was stone; it took the rats a long time, and some of them were crying with toothache before they had made so much as a tiny hole in the top of that box. And though they gnawed on and on, they couldn't make the hole big enough for one of them to creep inside and get the amber out.

So then the cat ran to find the king of the mice; and very frightened that little king was when the cat pounced on him.

'I am not going to hurt you, my friend,' said the cat, holding that little king firmly between her paws. 'But I want you to do something for me. And if you will do it, I will make a ten years' truce with you. I promise that during that time I will not so much as cast an eye on any of your subjects. And as for gobbling any of them up – no, nothing shall be farther from my thoughts!'

'Wh-what do you w-want me to d-do?' stammered the little king.

So the cat told him, and she carried little king mouse gently in her mouth up into the attic. She clambered with him on to the top of the clothes press, and pushed him through the little hole in the lid of the tobacco box.

Now little king mouse is scrabbling about inside the box. The cat is trembling with excitement. 'Is it there – is the amber there?' cries she. 'But of course it is, I know it is!'

'Yes, it's here,' squeaks little king mouse. 'But it's so big – so heavy – I can't lift it.'

'Rubbish!' snarls the cat. 'Remember the ten years' truce. Make an effort! If you don't make an effort, I'll – I'll *eat* you!'

Little king mouse did make an effort. And after a lot of scrabbling and panting, he came up through the hole, dragging the amber with him.

Who so happy now as dog and cat? They had but to carry the amber across the river, and all would be well again with them and with their dear old master – Though to cross the river they must wait until the last of the floating lumps of ice had melted; and the waiting was a sore trial. But there came a sunny day when the river was once more clear of ice, and on that day the cat took the amber in her mouth, and jumped on to the dog's back. And the dog plunged into the water and began to swim.

Swim, swim, swim – oh, what a long, long way it was across that river! Half way across, three quarters of the way across, legs aching, back aching, water in his eyes, in his ears, in his mouth: never mind for that . . . . Nearly across now, the quay almost within reach, and on the quay a little group of children, laughing at the funniest sight ever they saw in their lives.

'Ha! ha! ha! Oh see, oh see,' cried the children, 'a cat riding on a dog's back! Ha! ha! ha!'

And 'Ha! ha! ha!' laughed the cat, as excited as the children. 'Ha! ha! . . .' Oh me, oh me, when you laugh you open your mouth, and when you open your mouth you drop what is in it. Yes, the amber has fallen into the river. And down, down, down it goes.

The cat screams, the dog dives: down, down, down he goes after the amber. Has he got it? No, he hasn't. The cat, feeling herself to be drowning, digs her claws into his back: she hurts him so much that up he comes again. . . .

And when at last they reach the shore – oh, what a scene! The cat fleeing for her life, the dog after her yelping with rage; the cat scrambling up into a tree, dripping and spitting; the dog rushing round the tree, yelping, yelping. . . .

And that's how the old man found them: two angry, bitterly disappointed animals, whom he had a job to calm down and bring to their senses.

'It's all your fault,' snarled the dog to the cat.

'I couldn't help it!' sobbed the cat, safe in the old man's arms.

'Never mind, my children,' says the old man.

He is so glad to see them again that he doesn't seem to care a fig about the amber.

But the dog cares: every day he is out in the river, diving for that amber. But he can never find it – and his master is so poor, so poor! And then one day, just as he is about to plunge yet again into the water, he sees a man standing on the quay, fishing with a

rod and line. And some big fish which he has already caught are lying on the quay beside him.

'*Sniff! Sniff! Sniff!*' What is our dog smelling? Fish, yes, certainly; but also something else. The amber, the amber, it's the amber he is smelling, and the smell comes from inside one of the big fish!

'I'll pay you tomorrow!' barks the dog, snatches up that fish, and races home with it.

'Cut it open, master, cut it open!'

The old man takes a knife and slits the fish open. Sure enough, out drops the amber. Ah ha! Ah ha! What laughing, what shedding of happy tears, what rejoicing! But the old man's wine jug is empty and dusty. He must wash it. And then – what must he fill it with? Water? No: the amber will not change water into wine; it will only perfect and replace whatever liquid the jug contains. And what good is an ever overflowing jug of water? Be it never so pure, it will not rejoice the heart, nor will it bring in those pennies, and twopennies, and sixpennies we must have if we are to live.

So the old man takes the empty jug and his very last pennies, and off with him to the village, to buy a loaf of bread and some poor cheap wine to fill the jug. And before he goes he puts the amber in the empty chest where he had once kept his wealth.

'Guard well that chest, my darlings!' says he.

So the cat and the dog jump on to the chest and sit there. If a thief should come – let him look out!

But no thief came; and by and by the old man returned with the loaf of bread and the jug full of poor cheap wine. He cut the loaf into three; they all ate their share, but the cat and the dog turned up their noses at the wine. So the old man drank a little of it, and the rest he tipped away. Then he opened the chest to take out the amber, that he might drop it into the jug.

Glory! Glory! Glory! What does he see? All the money that he had ever put into the chest is now back in it. So is the dog's silver collar, and the cat's gold ball, and the old man's fine suit of clothes. For it was not only in the wine jug that the amber worked its magic. No; in whatever empty place it found itself, into that place it put back whatever had once been there. So our old man has now as much money as ever he needs, and wine to sell without end. Not that he needed to sell his wine, but the people clamoured for it. They came with their jugs and their bottles; and it was, 'Hey, old man, give us some of your good wine to carry home, that our days may be bright and our sleep calm and happy!'

So the countryside was full of happy people: but none more happy than our old man and his cat and his dog.

4 · The Flute Player

There was once a lad who had no little sweetheart. And Christmas came, and there was a feast. The other lads went with their sweethearts, but our lad thought, 'If I go alone I shall be laughed at.' So he stayed at home.

And he felt bored and lonely, and thought, 'What shall I do to pass the time?' So he took his flute and went to the bath house. And there he lit a candle and sat him down to play.

Ah, I tell you, that lad could play! He could bring tears to your eyes, or laughter to your lips, just as he pleased.

Well, he hadn't been playing long, when there came a maiden – though where she came from the lad didn't know. He played a merry jig and she began to dance. She danced towards him, she danced away from him, she danced round him, she danced up close to him and gave him a kiss. But when the clock struck twelve she vanished.

The next evening the lad went again to the bath house and played his flute. And again the maiden came and danced and kissed him, and vanished when the clock struck midnight. And the lad thought, 'What does it mean? I must ask my old godfather about this.'

So he went to his godfather and told him, and the godfather gave him a little cross on a chain. 'Hang this cross round your neck over your coat,' says he. 'Go again to the bath house and play your flute. And if again the maiden comes and stoops to kiss you, quickly take off the cross and hang it round her neck.'

The lad did that. He took his flute to the bath house and began to play. And sure enough by and by in came the maiden and danced to his playing. And when she came up close and stooped to kiss him, he had the little cross off his own neck and on to hers in a twinkling. . . . And then what happened? There came a shrieking from outside the window like all the cats in the world screaming together. And the lad was so frightened that he fell down in a faint.

When he came to himself it was morning. He was lying on the bath house floor, and the maiden was standing by his side.

'Who are you?' says he. 'Where do you come from? And what was that screaming outside the window?'

He asked her a lot of questions, but she answered never a word. So the lad hurried off home, and the maiden followed him and came after him into the kitchen.

And his old godfather was in the kitchen, having his breakfast.

'So you've brought her,' says he.

'Yes,' says the lad. 'But I think she's dumb.'

'Oh no, she's not,' says the godfather. And he took the maiden by her shoulders and shook her till her teeth rattled. 'Speak, you hussy, speak!' bawls he.

'Well then, I will speak,' says she, 'but leave me go. I don't know what I've done that you should treat me so!' And she began to weep.

And the lad put his arms round her and said, 'She's not to be frightened!'

So the old godfather said she must tell who she was, and why she came into the bath house. Because it wasn't maidenly to go kissing strange lads, and raising a din outside the window to scare people out of their wits.

'I didn't do that,' said the maiden. 'That was the witch girls.'

So then she told them that she was the daughter of a duke. But that eighteen years ago, when she was a baby, the witch girls had stolen her out of her cradle. They had left a changeling in her place, and she had lived with those witch girls ever since.

'And we were dancing outside the bath house one night,' says she, 'when we heard someone playing. And I wanted to go in and see who it was who played so sweetly. And they let me go. "Dance for him, tease him, plague him, pinch him black and blue," said they. But I couldn't do that to such a pretty lad, so I kissed him instead. And they were angry and called me out, and bade me go again next night to plague him. But you see I kissed him again. So they sent me in yet a third night; but he was cleverer than we were, this lad. He threw a charm round my neck, and then I couldn't get away. And they were caterwauling there under the window in their rage; but still I couldn't get away. So they flew off and left me. That charm has broken their power over me, and now I am free. So I will go back to my father's castle, and the lad must come with me.'

'Yes, he shall go with you,' said the godfather.

So they set out in a tumbledown cart drawn by an old donkey, for that was the best the godfather could provide. And they hadn't by a long way reached the duke's castle when the cart broke in two. And as for the donkey, he wouldn't walk a step farther. So they left him to find his way home, and walked on.

And when they came to the duke's castle, they weren't allowed in. But the maiden said, 'Hasn't the duke a little child?'

'Yes, that he has,' they told her.

'Well then,' says she, 'it's on that child's account we have come.' So then they were let in and brought to the duke.

The duke said, 'What do you know about that child, that you come pushing your way into my castle?'

'I know no more than this,' said she, 'that the child is eighteen years old, and neither speaks nor grows. But it is not your child at all, because I am your daughter.'

'*You* my daughter!' said the duke. 'How do you make that out?'

'Well,' says she, 'when I was a baby the witch girls stole me out of the cradle, and put this thing in my place.'

'You'll have to prove that,' says the duke. 'I'm not taking your word for it, though I'll own you're pretty enough.'

'Well then,' says she, 'didn't you, just after I was christened, give a feast?'

'I did so,' says the duke.

'And wasn't a silver ladle stolen from the table?'

'It was so,' says the duke.

'And didn't you blame the housekeeper for stealing it?'

'You're right about that,' says the duke.

'Well, it was the witch girls who stole it,' says she, 'and if you're doubting me, here it is.' And she snapped her fingers in the air, and the ladle fell down on to the table.

'And didn't you give another feast, and wasn't a silver beaker stolen from the table?'

'It was so,' says the duke.

'And you blamed the housekeeper again?'

'Yes, I did.'

'Well, the housekeeper didn't steal it, the witch girls did. And one of them had me in her arms and gave me the beaker to play with. And if you're doubting me, here it is.'

And she clapped her hands, and down fell the silver beaker on to the table.

'I think you must be my daughter,' says the duke.

'I surely am!' says she. 'And now that I've given you back your ladle and your beaker, you must give me this pretty lad for my husband; because he has freed me from the witch girls, and the best you have in the world isn't enough to repay him for that.'

'Well, you shall have him,' said the duke. 'But what am I to do with the ugly thing that's been eighteen years lying in the cradle?'

'Make a big fire in the courtyard,' says she, 'and bring me the creature.'

So they did that, and the girl took the hideous little creature in her arms, and went out into the courtyard, where the fire was blazing. 'I'm going to count three,' says she. 'And then – in it goes!'

'One,' says she, and swings the creature towards the fire. And there were the witch girls screaming round her head.

'Two!' says she, and gives the creature another swing towards the fire.

'Ah! Ah! Ah! Oh! Oh!' The witch girls were screaming louder and louder, and before the girl could give another swing, they had snatched the creature out of her arms, and put a log of wood in its place.

'Three!' cries the girl, and swings out her arms, and flings the log of wood into the fire.

'That's done with that,' says she to her father. 'And now we must hold our wedding.'

Well, she got her way over that, as over everything else. The girl and the lad were married that very day, and the duke gave them a grand house to live in. So the lad sent for his old godfather, and they all three lived happily to the end of their lives.

5 · The Dwarf with the Long Beard

In a far distant land a beautiful princess fell in love with a handsome prince, and he fell in love with her. So, followed by a great retinue, they set off for church to get married. But just as the wedding procession was about to enter the church, there came a blinding cloud of dust. For a moment no one could see anything. And when the dust cleared away, the princess had vanished. A dwarf with a long beard had carried her off.

The princess had fainted with terror. When she came to herself she was lying on a sofa in a magnificent room; and a table at her side was laden with food and drink in gold and silver dishes.

'Eat and drink!' said a voice.

Eat and drink indeed! The princess had never felt less like it! She ran to the door and tried to open it. But the door was locked, So she went back to the sofa again and burst into angry tears.

Then the door opened, and in came four huge men carrying a golden throne. On the throne sat a hideous dwarf, only seven inches high, with a beard seven feet long.

The huge men set down the throne at the princess's feet. The dwarf hopped from the throne on to the princess's knee, and tried to kiss her. But she struck him such a blow in the face that he toppled backwards, tripped over his long beard, and fell to the floor. So then the huge men picked him up, set him on his throne again, and carried him out of the room.

Now in his fall the dwarf had dropped a cap which he was holding in his hand. It was a very queer looking cap, and the princess put it on her head and ran to a looking glass to see how it suited her. What did she see in the looking glass? Nothing at all. For the cap was a magic cap and made its wearer invisible.

'Oh! Oh!' thought the princess. 'This is a treasure, and may help me to escape!'

She was amusing herself, taking off the cap and seeing herself in the glass, and putting on the cap and not seeing herself, when the door burst open and in ran the dwarf. He had his beard tied up with a thousand coloured ribbons – he wasn't going to trip over it again! But where was the princess? She had put on the cap, and she had vanished.

So, whilst the dwarf was searching for her under the sofa and behind the curtains, she ran out through the open door and into the garden, which was very large and beautiful.

In that garden the princess lived for some time, eating the fruit from the trees and drinking the water from the fountain. The dwarf was running about looking for her, and sometimes he heard her laughing. Sometimes, too, she would throw fruit stones in his face; and sometimes she took off the cap and showed herself for a moment. Then the dwarf would make a jump to catch her by the ankles, and she would give him a kick, put on the cap again, and away with her, laughing at him.

But one morning, when she had been thus teasing the dwarf and was scampering away, her cap caught in the branches of a thorn tree, and came off. There she was, plain to see!

'Rise up your branches, rise up your branches!' screamed the dwarf to the thorn tree. And the tree lifted its branches high into the air, lifting the cap with them. Now let the princess leap and stretch up her arms as she will – she can't reach that cap! The dwarf whistles to his four huge servants, they come running, they pick up the princess, carry her in, and lay her down on the sofa.

41

The dwarf clambers on to the sofa and breathes into her nostrils. She falls fast, fast asleep. No, nothing will wake her. And the dwarf puts the cap back on her head. Now she disappears. No, no one can see her.

'Oh ho, oh ho, my lady, you'll play no more tricks on me!' screams the dwarf. And he laughs till the room rings.

But what about the prince, whose bride had been snatched from him? Well, as soon as the dust cleared, he jumped on to his horse and rode off in search of her. He rode, rode, rode, asking everyone he met if they had seen the princess. But nobody had. And on the third day of his seeking, when he was resting by the wayside quite worn out, there came hobbling to him an old, old beggar woman.

'Alms, alms, good sir!' whined the old beggar woman. 'Will you spare a penny for a poor old soul who hasn't had a mouthful to eat, nor a sup to drink these many days?'

The prince gave the old woman a gold piece, and now she was laughing. 'One good turn deserves another,' says she. 'Do you want to find your princess?'

'Do I not!'

'Well then,' says she, 'call the dappled horse with mane of gold.' And having said that, the old woman vanished.

So then the prince knew she must be a fairy. He jumped to his feet and called, 'Dappled horse with mane of gold, come to me!'

Lightning flashed, thunder pealed, and down out of the clouds a horse came flying. My word, that was a horse! His coat was dappled white and silver, his mane was gold, his wings were gold; flames came from his nostrils, sparks from his eyes. 'What are your orders, prince?' said he.

'Help me to find my princess,' said the prince. And he told the horse all that had happened.

The horse said, 'Creep in at my left ear and come out at my right.'

42

'Oh, my horse, that is not possible!'

'Do as you're told,' said the horse, stamping a golden hoof. 'Everything is possible. Come, we are wasting time!' And he stooped his head into the prince's hand.

So then the prince crept in at the horse's left ear, and came out at his right. He came out clothed in a suit of shining armour. And he came out a hundred times stronger than he went in. When he stamped his foot and shouted, the earth trembled, and the leaves fell off the trees.

'Now,' said the dappled horse, 'up on my back. And you, little brother,' says he to the prince's own horse, 'wait here awhile and crop the wayside grass. You are not made for this adventure.'

The prince sprang on to the back of the dappled horse. 'Dappled horse with mane of gold, where are we going?'

'We go to seek the sharp-smiting sword with the never-failing blade,' answered the horse. 'For that is the only sword that will overcome the dwarf who has stolen your princess. You must know that the dwarf has a brother as huge as he himself is small. And it is in the keeping of this brother that we shall find the sword.'

Then the dappled horse spread his golden wings and rose into the air. Away, and away, and away, flying over hills and forests and swift-flowing streams, skimming low over prairies, rising high over mountains: away, away, away, till they came to a vast plain. And on the plain lay a giant turned into a mountain, with forests sprouting all over him. The giant's head, cut off from his body, lay like a huge round boulder cupped in his mossy hands. And beside the head lay the sharp-smiting sword with the never-failing blade.

The giant's eyes were closed, and the plain echoed with his snoring.

The dappled horse hovered in the air over the monstrous head. 'Prince,' said he, 'lean along my neck; we must snatch the sword before the giant wakes.'

43

The prince lay along the horse's neck, the horse swooped close, the prince snatched up the sword and gave a shout of triumph.

The giant's head opened its enormous eyes. It opened its enormous mouth. It spoke in a voice like the roaring of winds through an underground cavern: 'Little mannikin, are you weary of your life that you come here?' Then the enormous eyes caught sight of the sword in the prince's hands, and the eyes turned bloodshot with fear. 'Ah! Ah!' roared the voice, 'do not harm me! If you seek the dwarf with the long beard, you cannot hate him more than I do! He is my brother, and shamefully has he treated me! The sharp-smiting sword that you hold in your hand belonged to a magician who buried it deep under a mountain. And the dwarf came to me and said, "Brother, I know where the sharp-smiting sword is hidden. Let us dig it up, and possess it, lest the magician destroy us both." Well, I took the largest oak tree I could find, and with that oak tree raked up the mountain, and unearthed the sword. Then I said, "I have found the sword. It is mine."

'The dwarf said, "I told you where it was hidden, therefore it is mine."

'And so we came to quarrelling. And after we had quarrelled for a long time, the dwarf said, "Brother, to bandy words gets us nowhere. Let us each put an ear to the ground, and the sword shall belong to him who first hears the bells ringing from yonder church." Oh me, fool that I was – I put my ear to the ground. The dwarf swung the sword and cut off my head. But I roared so loud that he dropped the sword and fled. Now the sword is yours. Take it, cut off the beard of my wicked brother, for it is in his beard that his strength lies. Avenge my wrong, and after that do with me what you will!'

'You shall be avenged right speedily!' said the prince. And almost before the words were out of his mouth, the great eyes in the giant's head closed. There now – he's snoring again. And the horse flies with the prince to hover low over the dwarf's palace.

The dwarf is in his garden. He looks up, sees the hovering horse
and in rage and fear he seizes a dagger and springs high, high up
into the clouds. Now he will fall upon the prince out of the clouds
and stab him. But the dappled horse shouts, 'Look above you, my
prince!' The prince looks up, he sees the dwarf swooping down
upon him; he swings the sharp-smiting sword; it cuts through
the dwarf's beard, the beard tumbles to earth, and the dwarf
tumbles after it.

Yes, the dwarf is dead.

The dappled horse descends to stand by the dwarf's body.

'Brave work, my prince! Now down off my back. Pick up this seven inches of dead wickedness, and fasten it to my saddle bow. But take the beard and wrap it carefully round your arm, for you may have need of it. Then into the palace with you to find your princess!'

So the prince fastened the dead dwarf to the saddle bow, and with the beard wrapped round his arm, went into the dwarf's palace. And at the sight of that beard, the four huge men, the servants of the dwarf, fled howling. The prince went from room to room, searching and calling. 'My princess! My princess!' But let him call as he will, she does not answer.

'My princess, where are you? My princess, where are you?' He calls, calls, and the echoes mock him. Oh, what to do? He is desperate now, searching in every corner, opening cupboards, pulling out presses, overturning chests, peering under beds. 'My Princess, where are you?' He comes into a magnificent room, and in the room is a golden sofa. There is nothing on that sofa but a curious shaped cap. He seizes the sofa to drag it from the wall. Maybe there is a hidden door behind it! The sofa is heavy, he pulls and jerks. The cap rolls to the ground. . . . And lo! There on the sofa lies his princess, fast asleep.

'Oh, my princess, oh, my princess, wake, wake!' He takes her in his arms, he covers her face with kisses. She does not wake. So he puts the cap in his pocket and carries the sleeping princess out of the palace.

'She will not wake, my horse, she will not wake!'

'Ah,' says the dappled horse, 'the end is not yet. There is a way to wake her, but we do not know it. Come, we must go back to the giant.'

So the prince, with the sleeping princess in his arms, gets on to the back of the dappled horse once more. The horse spreads his wings, away they fly, away and away, and come to the plain where the giant's head, that huge boulder, lies beside the great mountain that is the giant's body.

The eyes in the giant's head are fast shut, and the plain echoes with his snoring. 'Wake up!' cries the prince. 'The dwarf is dead – here is his body!'

The giant's head opens its huge eyes, it opens its huge mouth. With one gulp that huge mouth swallows down the dwarf's body. It heaves an enormous sigh. 'Now I am satisfied,' it mumbles. 'Trouble me no more.' And the huge eyes close again.

'He will never wake from that sleep,' said the dappled horse. 'What is he but a mountain clothed with forest, and a boulder covered with moss?'

Then the dappled horse sprang into the air and flew on with the prince and the sleeping princess till he came to the place where the prince's own horse stood patiently waiting and cropping the road-side grass. 'Prince,' said the dappled horse, 'you are now but three days' journey from home. And here for the present we must part.'

'Oh no, my dappled horse!'

'Oh yes, my prince. I must go seek the fountain of wisdom. We have yet to learn how to waken the princess. When we meet again I may have news for you.'

So the prince, with the sleeping princess clasped in his arms, got on to his own horse, and the dappled horse flew away. The prince journeyed on. He rode, rode, rode, and now it was night. So he dismounted, wrapped the sleeping princess in his cloak, and laid her on the grass by the wayside. Then he lay down beside her, and fell asleep.

Ah, how tired he was! How soundly he slept! At dawn he was still sleeping, when a wicked knight came riding by. The knight draws his sword, stabs our prince, lifts the sleeping princess from the grass, and rides off with her to her father's palace.

'My lord and king,' says he to the princess's father, 'I have brought your daughter back to you. She was carried off by a terrible enchanter, who fought with me for three days and three nights before I slew him. Have I not truly won the princess for my bride?'

'My daughter, my little daughter!' The king with tears of joy, flung his arms about the princess. 'Wake, my darling, wake!'

But the princess did not wake.

The queen, the princess's mother, came running. She flung her arms about the princess. 'Wake, my darling, wake!'

But the princess slept on.

The court doctors were called. With their medicines and their unguents they dosed and anointed the princess.

But the princess did not wake.

'What is the meaning of it?' cried the king.

'That I cannot tell,' answered the wicked knight. 'As I found her, so you see her. But sleeping or waking, I claim her for my wife.'

What did it matter to him whether the princess slept or waked? To be her husband and heir to the throne was all he cared about. . . . And stretched on the grass by the roadside our prince lay bleeding from his wound.

'Is he dead? Is he dead?' cried the sparrows who hopped among the grass blades.

'Yes, I think he is quite dead,' chirped one.

'No, he is not quite dead,' chirped another, 'for there came a breath from his nostrils that fanned my feathers.'

'Then let us try to waken him!' chirruped a third.

And they hopped about him, pulling at his hair and chirruping in his ears, 'Wake up, prince! Wake up!'

The prince sighed, and opened his eyes. 'You see, you are not dead!' chirped the sparrows. And they flew off.

'Dappled horse, dappled horse with mane of gold, come to me!' moaned the prince.

Thunder pealed, lightning flashed; down from the clouds the dappled horse came flying. He stamped with his golden hoof, he breathed with his fiery breath into the prince's nostrils. 'Rise, prince, rise, your princess had need of you!'

Then the strong life that was in the dappled horse flowed up through the prince's nostrils and down into every atom of his body. And he rose up, whole and well.

'Mount, mount!' cried the dappled horse. 'At the fountain of wisdom I have learned how to waken the princess – if we are not now too late!'

So the prince leaped on to the horse's back. Away and away they flew to the king's palace. And the horse lighted down at the palace gates.

'You still have the dwarf's beard?' said the horse.

'Yes, it is wrapped about my arm.'

'One touch of that beard on the princess's forehead will waken her,' said the horse. 'You have the invisible cap?'

'Yes, it is in my pocket.'

'Put it on and hurry in. There is no time to lose!'

Then the dappled horse spread his wings and flew away, up into the clouds, and the prince put on the cap and passed unseen into the palace. What did he find? The king's councillors, assembled. The princess asleep on a couch. The wicked knight standing beside her. The king seated on his throne, reading from a parchment he held in his hand. 'Be it known to all present,' read the king, 'that wake she, or sleep she, I hereby declare that my beloved daughter shall be the wife of. . . .'

But the parchment was struck from the king's hand.

'Wake, my beloved, wake!' cried a voice. And snatching off the cap of invisibility, the prince stooped and touched the princess's forehead with the dwarf's beard.

The princess opened her eyes, she smiled, she rose up, she flung her arms about the prince.

'Ah, my prince!'

'Ah, my princess!'

'I don't understand!' cried the king. 'I don't understand any-thing!'

So then the prince told the whole story, and the king declared that the false knight should be plunged into boiling oil. But the knight had fled. Nor could they find him.

Well, let him go! Why fret our heads about a traitor? The happy, happy princess has her happy, happy prince. And this time, when they set out for church to be married, they meet no blinding cloud of dust to snatch them one from the other. The sun shines brightly, the bells ring out merrily. So, wishing them all happiness, we will bid them goodbye.

6 · The Hat

A lad was raking hay in his father's meadow. He looked up at the sky and saw dark clouds, far off, but steadily mounting and spreading. So he hurried on with his raking, and having finished his work, ran to get home before the storm broke. And on his way he saw a stranger fast asleep under a tree.

The lad took the stranger by the shoulder and shook him. 'Wake up, wake up!' he cried. 'There's a storm coming! If you stay here you'll presently be soaked to the skin!'

The stranger scrambled to his feet, rubbed his eyes, and glanced up at the threatening clouds. 'You're right!' said he. 'Where can I shelter?'

'Come to our farm with me,' said the lad. 'My people are at market, but I know they'd welcome you, were they home.'

So the two of them set off running. The sky grew blacker and blacker, the dark clouds covered it entirely, and the lad and the stranger had but just reached the farmhouse, when there came a flash of forked lightning that split the sky from end to end. On top of the lightning, without a moment's pause, came the roar of thunder and a deluge of rain, and looking back, as they darted through the farmhouse door into shelter, they saw the tree under which the stranger had been sleeping topple and crash to the ground.

'You have saved my life!' said the stranger to the lad.

He was a fine looking man, this stranger, tall and handsome,

with eyes the colour of forest leaves. But he limped a little and had one shoulder higher than the other.

Well, the lad set meat and drink before him, pushed up a chair to the kitchen fire, and bade him rest there tranquil till the storm had passed. The stranger smiled, but he said little. He looked into the glowing fire, as if he were reading a message there. So, after a while, the storm passed, and the stranger got up to go.

'Lad,' said he, 'my pockets are empty. I have nothing now with which to repay your kindness. But the day will come; yes, the day will come! Listen to me, and do not forget what I tell you. By and by you will enlist as a soldier. Oh yes, I know, nothing now is farther from your thoughts, but as I tell you, so it will be. You will find yourself a stranger in a foreign land; the years will pass. You will remember your home, and long, long to be back there. On the day when that longing becomes unbearable, look about you. You will see a crooked birch tree. Go to this tree, knock three times on the trunk and say, "Is the crooked man at home?" The rest will follow. And so for the present – farewell.'

And having so spoken the stranger vanished – leaving the lad, you may be sure, all agape with astonishment.

Well, it was not long afterwards that the king of the country went to war with the king of another country. And the king's men, with their papers and their long lists of names, came hammering on the farmhouse door. Willy nilly, they took away our lad to serve in the king's army, and sent him off to fight in a foreign land. And since the lad understood horses and was a fine rider, they dressed him in a fur hat and a wide thick coat, and put him into a cavalry regiment.

The war dragged on and on; four years passed; the lad grew more and more miserable. 'Shall I never see my home again?' he thought.

Ah, such sadness! Misery, wounds, blood, and death all round him: and there far, far away, the beloved farm; his father with no son to help him, his mother perhaps weeping as she moved about the house! 'I cannot bear it! I cannot bear it!' he thought. And he looked round him in desperation.

What did he see, a few paces ahead of him, but an old crooked birch tree. And at the sight of that tree, the words of the stranger, long forgotten, came back into his mind. 'He foretold all this,' thought the lad, 'I will do as he bade me.' And he went up to the birch tree and knocked on the trunk three times.

'Is the crooked man at home?'

Well, the words were scarcely out of his mouth when the tree opened, and out stepped the stranger. 'My friend,' said the stranger, 'I thought you had forgotten me. You are unhappy?'

'I am very unhappy,' said the lad.

'And you long to go home?'

'And I long to go home. Oh, how I long to go home!' said the lad.

The stranger turned to the crooked birch tree and called, 'Boys, boys, which of you can run fastest?'

And a voice from inside the tree answered, 'Father, I can run as fast as a grouse can fly.'

'Very good, but I want a quicker messenger today,' said the stranger.

Then another voice answered from inside the tree, 'Father, I can run as fast as the fastest wind.'

'Ah, but today I want someone even quicker.'

Then a third voice called from inside the tree. 'Father, I can run as fast as the thoughts of man.'

'It is you I want then,' said the stranger. 'Go, fill four big sacks with gold, and carry the sacks home with my friend and benefactor.' Then the stranger touched our lad's hat and said, 'Let the hat become a man, and let the man and the sacks go home!'

The lad felt the hat fall from his head. He turned to look for the hat, and – would you believe it? – there he was, dressed as a countryman, sitting in the farm kitchen, with four big sacks full of gold coins at his feet. And if his welcome was not the greater for those sacks full of gold, it was not the less.

Happily, happily they now lived: the lad, his mother, and his father; and their farm became one of the richest in the country.

But wasn't the lad arrested as a deserter? No, he was not. For in that faraway land, where the king's army was still fighting, a soldier, who was the exact image of our lad, wore his fur hat and his wide thick coat and rode his horse into battle. And when the war was ended, this man took off the hat and hung it on the crooked birch tree. Then he melted into nothingness.

The hat remained hanging on the birch tree all through the winter; and in the spring a bird came and made her nest in it. And a fine warm nest it was.

7 · Fedor and the Fairy

There was a lad, Fedor was his name, and he took a hunk of bacon and three big loaves of bread, and set out into the world to seek his fortune. So, when he had walked till he was weary, he came into a wood, and sat down to eat. And there came to him a handsome youth who said, 'Friend, I have been wandering all over the world. I am tired and hungry. Can you of your kindness spare me a morsel of food?'

'Help yourself,' says Fedor.

So the youth sat down by Fedor, and they ate together. Between them they ate one big loaf and a third of the bacon.

And when the youth got up to go, he gave Fedor an iron whistle. 'If you ever have need of me, blow this whistle,' said he. 'I am the King of the Winds.' And having said that, he vanished.

Fedor got up and walked on. Towards sunset he came to a great lake. And as he sat to eat, there came to him a youth in shining garments, who said he had been wandering far, far, far, and asked for food.

'Help yourself,' says Fedor.

So the youth in shining garments sat down by Fedor, and they ate together. Between them they ate up another loaf, and a third more of the bacon. And when the youth got up to go, he gave Fedor a golden whistle. 'If ever you have need of me, blow this whistle,' said he. 'I am the King of the Sun.' And having said that, he vanished.

Now it was evening. Fedor lay down under some trees near the lake, and thought to sleep. But the trees were rustling, rustling. And out from among the trees stepped a youth in silver garments, and asked for food. 'For I have a long way to go before morning,' said the youth.

So Fedor and the youth in silver garments shared the last of the bread and the last of the bacon. And when the youth got up to go, he gave Fedor a silver whistle. 'I am the King of the Moon,' said he. 'If ever you have need of me, blow this whistle.' And he walked away in a trail of soft silver light.

Fedor got up: no, he was not sleepy. He went to sit on the edge of the lake. The fishes were swimming in and out of the silver light that rested on the water. Fedor watched the fishes, and a voice said, 'What seek you here, where no one comes?'

Fedor looked up. At his side stood a beautiful maiden. 'I am a poor lad,' said he. 'I go to seek my fortune.'

'You need go no farther,' said the maiden. And she sat down beside him. They talked together until cockcrow, and then the maiden said, 'Fedor, I am a good fairy; if you are willing, I will take you to my house and marry you. But there is one thing I must tell you. From time to time I have to go out at night. And you must never, never ask where I go, or seek to follow me.'

'Your will shall be my will,' said Fedor, quite dazzled by her loveliness.

So the fairy took him by the hand – and how it happened I can't tell you – first they were by the lake, and next they were in a beautiful palace. And in that palace they were married, and lived together happily, oh so happily!

And always when Fedor went to sleep at night the fairy was at his side. And when he woke in the morning she was still at his side. By and by he forgot what she had said about going out at night – he thought no more of the promise he had given her. But one moonlight night he woke, and she was not there. He jumped out of bed, looked through the window. And saw her walking away from the palace – going where?

Ah, the fool! He ran out of the palace and followed her.

She walked fast, fast, he could not catch up with her. She came to the lake and sat on the shore. And the air was full of the sound of wings. A gigantic hideous bird, black as pitch, flew down from the sky. The fairy took the gigantic bird in her arms, she stroked the black feathers, she kissed the revolting head, she sang a tender lullaby that the bird might sleep.

Ah no! Ah no! Fedor could not, would not endure it! He snatched up a stick and rushed at the bird to kill it. But the bird gives a scream, lifts the fairy in his great talons, and flies away with her.

Fedor goes back to the palace, sick at heart. He waits, waits: his fairy wife does not return. He sets off to look for her. He wanders, wanders, up hill, down dale, and across the backs of mountains, calling, calling, 'My wife, my fairy wife, where are you?' But no one answers. Who will help him, who? He thinks of the King of the Winds, and of the winds that blow ceaselessly over the whole face of the earth. He takes the iron whistle out of his pocket and blows a long blast.

Then there came a rushing and a blustering in the air, and the King of the Winds stood before him. 'Fedor, what is your need?'

'Oh, King of the Winds, King of the Winds, a loathsome bird has stolen away my beautiful wife! I cannot find her! May it be that one of your winds has seen her?'

The King of the Winds snaps his fingers, and Fedor falls to the ground, for all the winds of the world come whirling round him. But no, not one of them has seen the great black bird, not one of them knows where Fedor's fairy wife is hidden.

So the King of the Winds flew off, and all his winds went with him, and there was a great silence. Then Fedor blew his silver whistle, and the King of the Moon, in his softly shining garments, stood before him.

'Fedor, what is your need?'

'A loathsome bird has stolen away my wife, I cannot find her!'

'Fedor, the last time I saw your wife was on the night you broke your promise. Where she is now, I know no more than you. Ask my brother, the King of the Sun, his eyes see farther than mine do.'

Then the King of the Moon walked away in a trail of silver light. Fedor blew his golden whistle, and the King of the Sun stood before him.

'Fedor, listen! I know what troubles you. The great bird

Takarana, who has carried off your wife, is nine-hundred-and-ninety-nine years old, and ripe to die. These many years he has laid a charm on your fairy wife, and compelled her every night to take him in her arms and sing her life-giving songs to him. You, in your foolishness, and forgetting your promise, sought to kill Takarana, and so he has carried your fairy wife away. Look now where I throw my light. What do you see?'

'I see an iron castle standing on a bare hill.'

'Fedor, your wife is inside that castle. The great bird Takarana has chained her to a pillar with seven iron chains. He thinks now that she will never escape him. But I with my heat can melt those chains. Call my brother, the King of the Winds, that whilst I shine hot on the chains, he may blow cold on your fairy wife that she be not burned.'

So Fedor blew his iron whistle again, and the King of the Winds came rushing. And the King of the Sun and the King of the Winds whirled off together to the iron castle, leaving Fedor to follow as fast as he could run.

And when Fedor reached the castle, the King of the Sun had already melted the chains, and Fedor's fairy wife came running out to meet him with icicles dripping from her hair, so fiercely cold had the King of the Winds blown upon her.

'Oh, my fairy wife! My fairy wife!'

Fedor took her in his arms, but she cried out, 'Alas! Alas! We cannot escape so easily! In one hour the great bird Takarana returns, and he will kill you and take me prisoner again!'

'Not so,' said the King of the Winds. 'I will summon all my winds to carry you away. Fedor, call the King of the Moon that he may lend you his mantle to ride on through the air.'

So Fedor blew his silver whistle, and the King of the Moon came bringing his silver mantle. And Fedor and his fairy wife, clinging together, sat down on the mantle. Then the King of the Winds snapped his fingers, and all the winds in the world came rushing. They blow with their mighty breaths; the mantle rises into the air – away it whirls high above the earth, fast, fast, faster.

But the great bird Takarana has come back to his iron castle; and when he finds his prisoner gone he lets out shriek after shriek, and he, too, rises into the air.

Fast, fast, faster: the mantle blown by the winds, the great bird chasing the mantle. All day, all night, for many days and nights, they whirl around the earth, the pursued and the pursuer. The sun lights them by day, the moon by night; the winds drive on the mantle. The great bird cannot quite catch up with his prey; but his prey cannot quite escape him. Nine times round the earth they whirl: but surely the great bird is quailing? He is nine-hundred-and-ninety-nine years old; he has no fairy now to take him in her arms and sing her life-giving songs to restore his youth to him. Let him flap his great black wings as he will, those great black wings will carry him no farther. His hour has come: and at sunrise on the tenth morning he gives a last terrible scream and falls to earth. See – he is dead.

Then the King of the Winds whispers to all the winds that blow, and they cease their blustering. Gently, gently, the moon mantle floats down to earth, and Fedor and his fairy wife step off it.

The King of the Moon hangs his mantle over his arm and walks off towards the west. The King of the Sun laughs and climbs up into the eastern sky. The King of the Winds whispers 'Goodbye', and tiptoes away over the fluttering grass blades. And Fedor and his fairy wife go back to their palace, and live there in happiness ever after.

8 · Pancakes and Pies

There was an old man and there was an old woman: poor – poor. They had no bread. They went to the forest to pick up acorns. They carried the acorns home to eat, and the old woman dropped one. The acorn fell through a crack in the floor, down into the cellar. It took root and grew down there. The old woman looked down through the crack in the floor and saw it – the little tiny oak tree!

'Old man,' says she, 'cut a hole in the floor, that the little oak tree may grow out. Then we shan't have to go into the forest to gather acorns, we can pick them up in our own kitchen.'

So the old man cut a hole in the floor, and the oak tree grew up into the kitchen. It grew, grew. It grew to the ceiling.

'Old man,' says the old woman, 'cut a hole in the ceiling.'

The old man cut a hole in the ceiling. The oak tree grew, grew. It grew till it reached the roof.

'Old man,' says the old woman, 'cut a hole in the roof.'

The old man cut a hole in the roof. The oak tree grew through it. It grew, grew, till it reached the sky.

'Old man,' says the old woman, 'take a sack and climb up the tree. Gather all the acorns that we may have a store against winter.'

The old man took a sack and climbed, climbed, climbed. He climbed right up into the sky. He got out of the tree and walked about the sky to see what was up there. He went, went, went about the sky, and there stood a little cock with a golden comb. And there stood a little handmill, sky-blue, with a gold handle. The old man didn't think any more about acorns. He picked up the little cock and the little handmill, and down the tree and in home again, fast as he could go.

'Here we are again, old woman! Is there anything to eat?'

'No, there isn't.'

Then the little cock with the golden comb stands on his tiptoes, stretches out his neck and sings out, '*Cock-er-ick-oo!* Try the handmill!'

So the old woman takes the mill and begins to grind. What comes out? Pancakes and pies! Would you believe it? No, you wouldn't. But out they come – pancakes and pies.

Pancakes and pies! Pancakes and pies! Oh ho! No more nibbling at acorns for our old man and woman! They are stuffing themselves full of pancakes and pies.

So when one day my lord duke is out riding, and feels hungry, and knocks at their door with 'Can you spare me something to eat?' it's 'Oh yes, my lord, oh yes!' And proud indeed is the old woman, turning her handmill, and grinding out pancakes and pies for his lordship.

'Well, old woman,' says my lord duke, 'that's the cunningest little contraption ever I did see! I'll give you a golden guinea for it.'

'Oh no, my lord, oh no, it's not for sale.'

'Two golden guineas then?'

'On no, my lord, oh no!'

Well, my lord duke may offer as many golden guineas as he likes: the old man and woman won't sell their handmill, and that's that. So what does my lord duke do? He turns ugly-tempered, slaps down a guinea on the table, snatches up the handmill, and rides off with it.

Oh, oh, oh! The old woman is sobbing, the old man is wailing. 'Our handmill, our lovely little sky-blue handmill with the golden handle! No more pancakes, no more pies, only acorns now for us to eat! Oh, oh, oh!'

63

'*Cock-er-ick-oo! Cock-er-ick-oo!*' The little cock is standing on tiptoe and stretching out his neck. 'I will fly! I will fly! I will overtake the wicked duke! I will peck him! I will claw him! I will get back our handmill!'

Off flies the little cock, fast, fast. But my lord duke is galloping fast, fast. My lord duke has a start of the little cock. He reaches his castle, jumps off his horse. In with him now, the handmill under his arm, and slamming the door behind him.

'*Cock-er-ick-oo! Cock-er-ick-oo!*' The little cock comes to alight on the castle gate. He stands on his tiptoes, stretches out his neck. '*Cock-er-ick-oo!* Duke, duke, give us back our handmill, our dear little sky-blue handmill with the golden handle!'

And the duke hears, and says to his servants, 'Catch that impudent bird and throw him into the water!'

The servants ran, they pounced, they snatched up the little cock, the beautiful little cock with the golden comb, and threw him into the well.

Down goes little cock, down under the water. But little cock is not dismayed. What is he saying? 'Little nose, little nose, drink up water! Little mouth, little mouth, drink up water!'

Little nose drinks, little mouth drinks; they drink up all the water.

'*Cock-er-ick-oo!*' Little cock flies up out of the dry well. He goes to perch on the duke's balcony. He stands on his toes, stretches out his neck. '*Cock-er-ick-oo!* Wicked one! Bad one! Duke! Duke! Give us back our handmill, our dear little sky-blue handmill with the golden handle!'

The duke says to his servants, 'Catch that impudent bird, and throw him into the burning stove!'

The servants run, they catch the little cock, the beautiful little cock with his golden comb, and they throw him into the burning stove.

Little cock is not dismayed. What is he saying? 'Little nose, little nose, pour out water! Little mouth, little mouth, pour out water!'

So little nose pours out water, and little mouth pours out water. They quench all the fire in the burning stove.

'*Cock-er-ick-oo!*' Little cock flies out of the wet stove. He flies, flies into the duke's dining hall. There sits the duke among his guests, turning the handmill, grinding out pancakes and pies. Little cock flies down on to the table. He stands on his toes, stretches his neck, '*Cock-er-ick-oo! Cock-er-ick-oo!* Thief! Thief! Duke! Duke! Give us back our handmill!'

'Ah! Ah! Oh! Oh!' The guests jump up from the table. No, thank you, they are not going to sit at table where such things happen: where little cocks with golden combs come talking at them, and little handmills grind out pies and pancakes! Leave such witchery to those who like it! They take to their heels and run out of the castle.

'Hey! Come back! Come back! I'll soon deal with that impudent cock!' The duke is running after his guests, waving his arms and shouting. What does little cock do? He snatches up the handmill, and flies away with it, back to the old man and woman.

'*Cock-er-ick-oo!* Here you are, my darlings! I've brought you back your little sky-blue handmill with its golden handle. Grind away, grind away, let's eat our fill of pancakes and pies!'

Pancakes and pies! Pancakes and pies! The old woman is laughing, the old man is laughing. The old woman takes the handmill and begins to grind. Out they come, pancakes and pies, more and more and more! The old man gobbles, the old woman gobbles, the little cock gobbles.

Ha! ha! ha! No more nibbling at acorns! No more feeling hungry and growing thin! Now we are growing fat, fat, fat, eating our fill of pancakes and pies!

9 · The Forty Goats

A king had three beautiful daughters, and the time came for those daughters to get married. But the princesses had so many suitors that neither they nor the king could decide which would make them the best husbands. So the king sought counsel of a soothsayer.

The soothsayer read in his Book of Destiny. And the words of the book were these:

Let the three princesses stand on the palace balcony, and let all the suitors stand below. Let each princess in turn throw her handkerchief down amongst the suitors. On whomsoever's head the handkerchief falls, that is the princess's destined mate.

So the three princesses went to stand on the balcony, each one holding her handkerchief. The princes, lords, dukes and earls, who were the princesses's suitors, stood under the balcony; and the great square in front of the palace was crowded with a throng of townsfolk come to see on whose lucky heads the handkerchiefs would fall.

Well, the eldest princess threw down her handkerchief: it fell on the head of a prince, young and handsome. And the crowd cheered.

The second princess threw down her handkerchief: it fell on the head of a duke, young, brave, and good. And the crowd cheered.

The youngest princess threw down her handkerchief. Where did it fall? Oh dear me, it fell on to the horns of a billy-goat that had pushed his way in among the suitors.

The crowd of townsfolk didn't cheer this time. They laughed.

'Take that handkerchief off the creature's horns,' said the king irritably. 'Hand the handkerchief up here. The princess must throw again!'

So the princess threw again. Where did the handkerchief fall this time? On to the horns of the goat.

And the crowd laughed more loudly.

'Drive that creature away!' cried the king. 'And hand up the handkerchief!'

So they drove the billy-goat away, and handed up the handkerchief, and the youngest princess threw once more.

What happened? The handkerchief went fluttering up and down in the air as if a breeze was blowing it: it hovered this way and that way over the heads of the suitors; it rose and fell, wheeled, and turned round and round in the air. Was it never going to fall? The excited crowd shouted and cheered. . . . But see, the billy-goat has pushed his way back among the suitors. What does the handkerchief do now? It drops swiftly down on to the goat's horns.

Then the crowd burst into such a roar of laughter that the palace walls echoed. The king took the youngest princess by the hand and hustled her back into the palace. 'We have been made a laughing stock!' said he. 'It is not my fault or yours. It is meant to tell us that you will never marry, but must remain a maiden all your life.'

The youngest princess wept. 'I do not wish to remain a maiden all my life!' said she. 'I would rather marry the billy-goat if such is my destiny.'

The king sent for the soothsayer again. The soothsayer opened his Book of Destiny and read. What did he read in the book this time?

The youngest princess shall marry the goat.

'Is that truly so?' said the king.

68

'That is truly so,' said the soothsayer.

So they held a triple wedding. The eldest sister married her prince, the second princess married her duke, and the youngest princess married the billy-goat.

But after the wedding, when the billy-goat and the princess were alone together – what did that billy-goat do? He gave himself a shake; his goatskin fell to the ground, and there, standing in front of the princess, was the handsomest lad ever you set eyes on.

'Oh! Oh! Oh! Who are you?'

'I am your goat, my princess. But I am also prince of the Eastern Isles, condemned by an evil sorcerer to take the shape of a goat. It is only when we are alone together that I may take my true shape. Now it remains with you, my princess, to make sure that we shall never be separated.'

'But what must I do?'

'Keep my secret,' said the prince. 'On the day that you tell anyone that I am other than a goat, on that day you will lose me for ever.'

'I will keep your secret, my husband,' said the princess. 'I will never, never tell.'

So the princess lived happily. When they were alone together, she had her handsome husband; but all that anyone else saw of him was a shaggy goat. And the people about the palace marvelled. 'How can our princess so love that ugly creature?' they whispered. 'But there, poor young thing, she has nothing else to love.' And they pitied their little princess, who, did they but know it, was happy as the day was long.

Now it so happened that a neighbouring monarch declared war on the king, the princesses's father; so he must summon his soldiers and send them out to fight. And he gave the command of the army to his two sons-in-law, the husbands of his two elder daughters. And the king's army defeated the enemy and came marching home in triumph. So then the king decreed a three days' fête, with feasting for all his people and sports and dancing. And on each of the three days, the fête was to open with a grand march of the whole army past the palace windows.

On the first day of the fête, the three princesses came out and stood on the balcony to watch the army march past.

'Here comes my prince at the head of the army!' cried the eldest princess. And she threw a red rose down to him.

'And here comes my duke marching beside him!' cried the second princess. And she threw a yellow rose down to her duke. 'But who is that young fellow marching so close behind them?'

'A stranger,' said the eldest princess. 'Someone, no doubt, who fought bravely in the battle.'

But look – what is the youngest princess doing? She is taking a white rose from her girdle and throwing it down to this same young fellow.

'You minx!' cried the eldest princess.

'Be ashamed of yourself, throwing flowers to strange young men!' cried the second princess.

But the youngest princess only laughed.

So the first day of the fête was spent in feasting and merriment, and the second day came; and again the army marched past the palace windows. And again the three princesses stood on the balcony to watch.

The eldest princess threw down her red rose to the prince, her husband. The second princess threw down her yellow rose to the duke, her husband. And the youngest princess took a sprig of jasmine from her belt, and threw it down to the young fellow who marched just behind the prince and the duke.

'Have you taken leave of your senses?' cried the eldest princess. 'You, with royal blood in your veins, behaving like any common little flirt!'

'The king, our father, should be told of this!' cried the second princess.

But the youngest princess only laughed.

So the second day of the fête passed, and the third day came, and again the three princesses stood on the balcony to watch the army march past. The eldest sister threw down her red rose to the prince, her husband. The second princess threw down her yellow rose to the duke, her husband. And the youngest princess took a white lily from her belt and threw it down to the young fellow who marched behind the prince and the duke.

And the young fellow caught the lily, and looked up at the balcony and smiled.

'Ah! Ah! Ah!' The two elder princesses were beside themselves with rage. They called their youngest sister every bad name under the sun. The youngest princess only laughed. So then the two elder princesses ran to tell the king how their sister was behaving.

And the king sent for the youngest princess.

'What is this I hear?' said he. 'A princess, my daughter, throwing flowers to strange young men! And you married, too! Even if your husband is only a goat that is no excuse for you to go flirting with strangers. Are you sorry for what you have done?'

No, the princess was not sorry.

'Then I will make you sorry!' blustered the king. 'You shall be locked up and fed on bread and water until you admit the error of your ways.'

But the princess answered proudly, 'My goat and I will not mind being locked up and fed on bread and water.'

'Your goat, your goat!' shouted the king. 'It must be living with that filthy creature that has made you forget your manners and your morals. I will have the creature killed!'

So then the princess fell on her knees and wept. 'Let me but keep my goat, oh, let me but keep him, and I will never offend again!'

But the king had now got it into his head that it was all due to her living with a goat that had made the princess behave as no

princess should. 'The butcher shall kill the creature this very day!'
he shouted.

Ah, what could the poor princess do? She begged and prayed
for the life of her goat. But the king would not listen to her. So at
last, with tears and sobs, she told him the whole story. She had
but thrown down the flowers to her own dear husband, she said.

'Well, why couldn't you have told me that before?' said the
king. 'But it's the strangest story that ever I heard! Come now, my
girl, give me a kiss and we'll say no more about it.'

'And you'll keep my secret?' said the princess.

'Yes, I'll keep your secret,' said the king. 'No one shall know
but our two selves.'

So the princess kissed her father and ran up to her room. Did
she think to find her goat there? Well, if she did, she didn't find
him. The room was empty.

'My goat, my goat!' cried the princess. 'Come to me! I had to
tell my father or he would have killed you! But he will keep our
secret, my goat!'

None came. None answered.

'He will come this evening,' said the princess. And she sat down
and waited. But no goat came.

'He will come tonight when all the palace sleeps,' said the
princess. 'I will wait and watch.'

But the night passed, and it was morning. And none came. The
princess ran through the palace crying, 'My goat, my goat! Who
has seen my goat?'

Nobody had seen him. And the days passed. And the goat did
not come.

So then the princess fell ill, and lay on her bed with closed eyes.
The king sent for his royal physician. The physician tried this
medicine and that medicine. No good. 'She is dying of love,' said
the royal physician. 'She must be roused and forget her sorrow.'

'Ah, but how to rouse her?'

'Send for all your story-tellers,' said the royal physician. 'Let them tell their stories – sad stories, merry stories, stories to make the hearer laugh or weep.'

So the king sent for every story-teller in the kingdom. One after another they came and sat by the princess's bed. They told their stories – merry stories; but the princess did not laugh; sad stories, but the princess did not weep. Always she lay with closed eyes as if she did not hear. . . .

Now there lived in a village near the king's city a poor old woman. And one day this poor old woman tucks up her petticoats, takes a stick in her hand, and sets off walking towards the city.

And a neighbour meets her and says, 'Whither away?'

'To the palace to tell the princess a story,' says the old woman.

The neighbour laughs. '*You!* What story have you to tell a princess?'

'I don't know yet, but I'll think of something as I go along,' says the old woman. 'And even if it doesn't make the princess laugh or cry, I hear the king will give a golden guinea for the telling of it – and that's worth having!'

'Well, I wish you luck,' says the neighbour.

And the old woman trudges on her way.

But the way was long, and the old woman got tired, and she sat down by a milestone to rest, and to think up some story to tell the princess. And as she so rested – what did she see? She saw, coming along the road, a golden cock drawing a little cart piled up with fruit and vegetables.

The old woman stared and gaped. And the golden cock came up to the milestone and struck it with his foot. Did you ever? The milestone turned over on its side and rolled away, and there was a gaping hole, and a passage going down into the earth.

The cock went down into the passage, drawing the little cart behind him. 'Hey! Hey!' cries the old woman, 'wait for me!' and she catches hold of the back of the cart, and down she goes after the cock.

73

Down, down, down – and where did she come to at last? Into a huge kitchen with saucepans bubbling on a big stove, and the smell of meat roasting in the great ovens.

Ah, the good smells! The old woman tiptoed about, sniffing here, snuffing there. The cock had disappeared; there was no one in the great kitchen but herself, and oh, but her mouth was watering! 'Well then,' thinks she, 'couldn't we just have a little taste of something?' And she took down a ladle from a peg on the wall, and lifted the lid on one of the saucepans. Soup, ho! ho! And soup, by the smell of it, fit for a king's table! This old woman is in luck! A little sip, a little sip, no one will miss just a little sip!

But even as she was about to dip the ladle into the soup, something slapped her hand, the ladle dropped to the floor, and a voice cried out, 'We do not touch until the mistress comes.'

The old woman scuttled out of the kitchen faster than fast; she went along a passage and came to a pantry; and on the pantry shelves were rows of freshly baked loaves – and oh, but the old woman felt hungry! 'Well then, if I can't have soup I'll have bread,' thinks she; she reaches out her hand to take a loaf. But no sooner had she touched the loaf than something gave her a smack in the face, and a voice cried out, 'We do not touch until the mistress comes!' And the old woman ran out of the pantry in a fright.

She ran and she ran; she didn't know now where she was going. She ran through rooms that were all lit up, and each one grander than the other; and she came at last into a great hall. In the middle of the hall was a big marble basin, filled up with sparkling water; and round the basin stood forty chairs, thirty-nine of silver and one of gold. And on every chair was a silken cushion, so plump, so soft looking that the old woman longed to sit her down and rest.

'Well, and why not sit down and rest?' thinks she. And she is just about to sit in the golden chair when she hears far off, but coming nearer and nearer, a sound like the clitter-clatter of many little hoofs walking on stones. 'Oh, oh!' thinks the old woman, 'maybe it's demons coming!' And she creeps under a divan against the wall, and crouches still as a mouse.

Clickerty, clickerty, clickerty, clickerty, click, click, click! The sound of little hoofs getting louder and louder. The sound is in the hall itself now. The old woman peers out from under the divan. What does she see? Thirty-nine goats scampering round the hall; and a fortieth goat, who wears a diamond crown, carried on the back of the thirty-ninth. One after another the goats plunged into the marble basin. . . . Yes, forty goats plunged into that marble basin, and came out again, and shook the water from their hides. And even as they shook themselves those hides fell off – and there, taking their seats in the thirty-nine chairs of silver, and the one of gold, were forty noble youths. And he who sat in the golden chair wore a diamond crown.

So for a time all the forty youths sat silent; then he who wore the diamond crown began to weep. And ever between his sobs he cried out, 'Oh, princess, oh, princess of grace and beauty! Oh, princess, oh, my princess!'

And all the thirty-nine youths wept also. 'Oh, princess! Oh, princess!' they sobbed.

And 'Oh, princess! Oh, princess of grace and beauty!' echoed the walls.

'Oh, princess! Oh, princess of grace and beauty!' Up from the floor, down from the ceiling, sounding from the great doors, crying from the windows, rising from the very furniture itself the sobbing echoes took up the lament. It was so sad, so very, very sad, that the old woman began to weep herself. Yes, the tears were streaming down her wrinkled face as she crouched under the divan. . . . And then suddenly all was silent; the lights in the hall went out, and the old woman found herself sitting once more beside the milestone.

'Well,' says she, getting up and shaking down her petticoats, 'here's a story to tell the princess! And if this story don't make her open her eyes, nothing ever will!'

So off with her, fast as she could trot, to the palace.

The princess lay on her bed with her eyes shut. The old woman came in clearing her throat, '*Hem! hem!*' and stamping her feet, *stump, stump,* to make a little clatter. But the princess did not open her eyes, nor make one movement.

'Well, my dear,' says the old woman, sitting down by the bed, 'you may think you're sad, and you may think you're in a bad case, but I know someone sadder and in a worse case than yourself. Now then, dearie, you listen to me. The beginning of what I have to tell you may make you laugh; but the end will surely make you cry.'

And the old woman began her story. She told about the golden cock drawing the little cart. But the princess took no heed. She told of the big kitchen, and of how the ladle had been struck out of her hand when she tried to taste the soup. She told of the pantry full of bread, and of how something had smacked her in the face when she made to pick up a loaf. She acted out her story with frowns and laughs and clapping of her hands. . . . Oh dear me, she might have been talking to a dead woman!

But when the old woman told of how she came into the big hall and heard the patter of goat's hoofs, the princess opened her eyes and sighed. And when the old woman told of the forty goats and one of them wearing a diamond crown, the princess sat up and burst into tears. And when the old woman told of how the goats bathed in the marble basin, and then shook themselves and shed their skins, the princess rose from the bed. And when the old woman told of the youth who wore the diamond crown weeping and lamenting, and of the words he had spoken, the princess grasped the old woman by the arm and cried out, 'Oh, take me to him, old woman! Take me to him!'

'Lordy, lordy,' says the old woman, 'so you've come to your senses at last! Of course I'll take you to him, only stop screeching at me, and get your clothes on! Put on a warm cloak too, and if you've a spare one I'd be glad of it myself, for it's coming on night time, and how do I know how long we may have to wait by the milestone?'

So they set out, the two of them. And they did have to wait by the milestone. They waited there all night, and the princess was in a frenzy of impatience, and the old woman coughed and scolded and wished the princess to the devil and herself back in her own little cottage. But at last the dawn came; the sun rose, and in the light of the rising sun – there was the golden cock, stepping along the road, drawing his little cart.

And it happened now as it had happened before. The cock struck the milestone with his foot. The milestone turned over on its side and rolled away; there was the passage going down into the earth; the cock, drawing his little cart, went down the passage, and the princess and the old woman followed him, and came into the big kitchen.

Oh, what good smells, oh, what merry sounds! The fire in the stove crackled as if it were laughing, the soup in the saucepans bubbled as if it were singing, and out of the oven came such cheerful sizzlings as made the old woman skip for joy. The old woman took down the ladle from its peg on the wall, dipped it into the soup. No one struck the ladle out of her hand; only a voice whispered in her ear, 'You may sup your fill – the mistress has come!'

'De-lic-ious!' The old woman smacked her lips. 'Take a sup of this, dearie!' says she to the princess.

But the princess had already run through the kitchen and was hurrying down the passage, so the old woman sighed and followed her. They came to the pantry where the freshly baked loaves were stacked upon the shelves. The old woman stretched up and took down a loaf. No one slapped her in the face; only a voice whispered in her ear, 'You may eat your fill – the mistress has come!'

'Oh, dear me, the old woman would have stayed in that pantry all day, eating her head off, but the princess was running on, and the old woman had to follow, chewing on her loaf as she went. So they passed through all the lit-up rooms, each one grander than the other, and came at last into the great hall, with its big marble basin filled up with sparkling water, and its forty chairs, thirty-nine of silver and one of pure gold.

But the great hall was empty and silent, and the princess burst into tears. 'He's not here! He won't come!' she sobbed.

'Oh, yes, he will, my pretty,' said the old woman.

Clickerty, clickerty, click, click, click: the sound of many little hoofs walking on stones. The old woman drags the princess to hide under the divan. In come the forty goats – ah, that one who wears a diamond crown – the princess would know him anywhere! Now she would cry out 'My husband! My husband!' and run to fling her arms about him, but the old woman whispers, 'Hush, you foolish girl!' claps one hand over the princess's mouth, and with the other hand holds her firm.

The goats bathe in the marble basin, they throw off their skins; thirty-nine handsome youths take their seats in the silver chairs, the fortieth – he who wears the crown – seats himself in the golden one. Ah, how he weeps! 'Oh, princess, oh, princess of grace and beauty!'

But – how's this? The thirty-nine youths, who sit in the silver chairs, are not weeping with him – they are laughing!

Ha! ha! ha! Ha! ha! ha! The walls echo the laughter. Up from the floor, down from the ceiling, sounding from the doors, flung back from the windows, rising from the very furniture itself, comes laughter, laughter, laughter! And still laughing, the thirty-nine youths leap from their silver chairs and run out of the hall.

The prince too gets up from his chair; he looks about him as one in a dream; the old woman lets go her hold of the princess, the princess comes out from behind the divan, she runs to the prince, she flings her arms about him. 'Oh, my husband, my husband,' she cries. 'Indeed I could not help it! I had to tell the king, or he would have killed you!'

Well, well, never mind about that now. They are in each other's arms, they are laughing and kissing. The prince of the Eastern Isles will never turn into a goat again. Yes, the spell is broken – and who has broken it? Why, our old woman to be sure! For it is she who has seen the prince both in the shape of a goat and in his true form, and has not told anyone that the prince is the goat, or the goat the prince, but has just put two and two together. All honour to the old woman!

The thirty-nine youths, who are the prince's thirty-nine companions, come laughing back into the hall, and . . . hey presto!

79

There they are, the whole troop of them, standing in the road beside the milestone.

And so they go back to the palace, and the princess runs to present her handsome husband to the king her father. What rejoicings, what fêtes and feastings! They keep it up for seven days and seven nights. And as to the old woman – they can't make enough of her! 'You shall live in the palace all your life,' says the princess. 'And when my children are born, it is you who shall be their nurse!'

Maybe! Maybe! But the old woman wasn't happy in the palace. Indeed she grew sadder and sadder. She was sighing and moaning all day long. And the princess said, 'What is the matter, my dear old woman, that you sigh and groan?'

What's the matter indeed? The old woman wants to go home, that's what's the matter. No, nothing else will please her. So at last they send her home.

The old woman goes into her poor little house and slams the door. What is she doing now? Hopping and skipping about her kitchen, clapping her hands and singing:

> '*Oh, my little house, my own little house,*
> *There's no place on earth like my own little house!*
> *So your kings may live in mazes,*
> *And your queens may go to blazes,*
> *For I'm home, home, home in my own little house!*'

10 · The Ogre, the Sun, and the Raven

There was once a bad wicked ogre who stole the sun out of the sky and put it in a box. Then the world went dark; the birds didn't sing, the flowers didn't bloom, and every one was miserable. So the birds went to their king, Raven, and said, 'Mighty King Raven, get us back our sun!'

Raven was very clever, and he'd been studying magic for some time. Now he sat in the dark and thought and thought. And then he spread his wings and flew off to the ogre's house.

The ogre was away, prowling about the dark world, stealing people's horses. So Raven flew down the smoke-hole into the ogre's house, and there was the ogre's baby lying in the cradle. Raven snatched up the baby and flew with it, away and away, till he came to the tall forest tree where his nest was. He had three little ones of his own in the nest, and he pushed the ogre's baby in with them. Then he turned himself three times round on his toes, muttered some spells, and changed the ogre's baby into a raven chick.

'Here's another little one for you to mind,' says he to his wife. And then he flies back to the ogre's house, and down the smoke-hole again.

What does he do next? He stands on the edge of the cradle, turns three times round on his toes, mutters some spells, and changes himself into a baby, so like the ogre's baby that you couldn't tell the difference.

So when the ogre comes home, there's the baby in the cradle. And isn't it yelling!

'*Wha-a-a!*' yells the baby. 'I want the sun to play with!'

'Well, you can't have it,' snaps the ogre.

'*Wha-a-a!* I want the sun! I want the sun!'

'Be quiet before I lerrup you!' shouts the ogre.

'*Wha-a-a!* I want the sun! I want the sun to play with!'

'Here's a rattle for you,' says the ogre. 'Play with that.'

The baby throws the rattle in the ogre's face. '*Wha-a-a!* I don't want the nasty rattle! I want the sun! I want the sun to play with!'

All day long that baby went on shrieking. The ogre tried slapping

it, he tried cuddling it, he tried giving it this, that, and the other. But it screamed and kicked and flung itself about, and all the time it was yelling out, '*Wha-a-a-a!* I want the sun! I want the sun to play with!'

The ogre went to bed and muffled his ears in a blanket. The baby went on yelling. It was still yelling when the ogre got up in the morning – it wanted the sun, it wanted the sun, it wanted the sun to play with! So at last the ogre took the sun out of its box, and flung it into the cradle. And then the baby stopped yelling and chuckled.

Well, after a while the ogre went out to feed the horses he had stolen. What did the baby do then? It jumped out of the cradle, turned three times round on its toes, muttered some spells and changed back into King Raven. And King Raven took the sun in his beak and flew up to the smoke-hole.

But, oh, dear me, the sun's so big, it won't go through the smoke-hole, however much Raven pushes and prods it. Raven pecks at it with his beak, he pecks off little pieces all round the edge of the sun, and tosses those little bits up through the smoke-hole. Away they float, up and up, right into the dark sky, and there they stay sparkling and twinkling. And the birds looked up and said, 'Oh, see, how pretty: little stars twinkling in the black sky, and that's better than utter darkness!' One or two birds tried to sing then; but the rest said, 'No, we can't sing till the sun shines again.'

And all this time Raven was prodding and pushing at the sun, and breaking off more and more bits to make it the right size to go through the smoke-hole. And at last with a mighty heave he did get it through; and up it rose, and up it rose, higher and higher into the brightening sky, putting out the stars with its blinding rays and lighting the whole world. Then all the birds burst into song, and the flowers bloomed again, and everyone was happy.

Raven flew back to his nest. There were four little ones in the nest now, his own three and the ogre's baby. They all looked exactly alike, but Raven knew which was the ogre's baby by the way it was behaving. It was squawking and pecking the other three, and trying to pitch them out of the nest. Mother Raven was having a bad time, trying to keep it in order.

'A good thing you've come back,' says she to King Raven. 'I'm losing my temper with this brat, that I am! And once a temper is lost it isn't so easy found again.'

So Raven stood on the edge of the nest, turned himself three times round on his toes, muttered some spells, and changed ogre nestling back into ogre baby. And he snatched up ogre baby and flew with it back to the ogre's house, and down through the smoke-hole, and dumped it into the cradle. It began to yell then, '*Wha-a-a! Wha-a-a-a!*' But Raven flew away and left it yelling.

So the baby was yelling inside the house, and the ogre was yelling outside the house, because he had just come out from his dark cattle-shed and seen the sun back in the sky. 'I'll have you down again, I'll have you down again!' he yelled, shaking his fist at the sun.

But he hasn't managed to get the sun down again yet. And it's more than likely that he never will manage it.

11 · Peppi

Now I'll tell you about Peppi. He has a widowed mother and two sisters. They can earn their living by spinning; but Peppi can't get work. Bah! That's hard. It makes Peppi frown.

So he goes to his mother and says, 'Mother, listen to what I say. I'm off to wander through the world.' And he goes.

He goes, goes; he comes to a farmhouse. He knocks, they open. 'Do you want a boy?' . . . But what to do if they don't want him? The thought makes him frown. He doesn't look very pleasant.

So what's the answer? They call the dogs. 'Hey, dogs, dogs, drive this fierce-looking fellow away!' The dogs rush out barking. Peppi walks off.

He goes, goes. He comes to a farm labourer's cottage. Knocks. 'Do you want a boy?'

What answer? 'Oh, come in! He who wants work needn't go away. Tomorrow I will ask the master.'

In the morning the farm labourer goes to the master. 'There is a boy come who wants work.'

'Well, give him some food. I will see about it.'

The farm labourer went back to his cottage. He gave Peppi a plate of bread and a bowl of buttermilk. Peppi ate. He was smiling.

The master went to his oxherd. 'Oxherd, you said you wished to leave me?'

'So I do.'

'Go then, I can get another oxherd.'

The oxherd went. The master came to Peppi. 'Peppi, you are

now my oxherd. Tomorrow you will go out with the oxen. But listen, my boy, it's like this. I will give you food, but nothing else.'

Peppi said, 'So be it. It is as God wills.' But now he's frowning again.

In the morning, Peppi went out with the oxen. He took with him plenty of bread and something to put on it. In the evening he brought the oxen back to the cattle-sheds. He did this day after day, till there came the time of carnival. On the first evening of carnival, when Peppi drove the oxen back to the sheds – oh, wasn't he scowling!

The master said to him, 'Peppi!'

'Oh?'

'What's the matter, Peppi, that you scowl so?'

'Nothing!'

Peppi went to bed. The fierce look was still on his face. And when he got up in the morning the fierce look was still there. He drove out the oxen, he brought them back to the sheds at night. He was still wearing his fierce look.

The master said, 'Peppi!'

'Oh?'

'What's the matter?'

'Nothing.'

'Nothing, Peppi? Come, you had better tell me!'

'What have I to say? Now it is carnival time. And I have not even a sixpence to give to my mother and sisters that they may make a feast.'

'Peppi, you have all that you need, except money. If you want bread for your family, take as much as you like.'

'But if I want to buy a little trifle of meat or sweet for my people, with what can I buy it?'

'Peppi, I have nothing more to say to you. You made the agreement with me. Now you must stick to it.'

'Oh.'

Next morning Peppi went out with the oxen. He sat down amongst them. He was scowling fiercely. And as he so sat, he heard a gentle voice call, 'Peppi! Peppi!'

Peppi looks round. Only the oxen.

'Peppi! Peppi!'

He looks all about him. Only the oxen. 'Eh, am I dreaming?'

'Peppi! Peppi!'

'Yes, but who calls me?'

An old ox turns round. 'Peppi, I called you.'

'*What!* You spoke!'

'Yes, why not? But what's the matter that you must always be scowling?'

'How should I not scowl? Here it is carnival time. I ought to be treating my mother and my sisters. But the master gives me nothing.'

'Peppi, listen to me. When you go home tonight say to the master, "What! Won't you even give me that old ox?" When he sees me, old as I am, and past work, he will give me to you.'

That evening Peppi went in with a scowl on him like the scowl of seven dogs.

The master said, 'Peppi, Peppi, why must you always scowl?'

Peppi said, 'You give me nothing. Won't you even give me that old ox, who has more years than any owl? I might at least skin it and make a stew of its tough flesh.'

The master said, 'Take it then. Take a piece of rope and lead it away.'

Next morning Peppi rose before dawn, took a piece of rope, took a knapsack, put eight loaves in it, sat himself on the back of the ox, and off with him.

They went, went, they came to a great plain. And a man on horseback came galloping towards them. The man cried out, 'Look to yourself! Look to yourself! There is a great bull coming, a bull that kills!'

The ox said to Peppi, 'If I take that bull, will you give him to me?'

Peppi said, 'For God's sake! You won't be able to take him! He will kill you!'

The ox said, 'Peppi, put yourself behind me. Don't you fear.'

Peppi got behind the ox. Up rushed the bull, head down, nostrils wide, legs galloping. *Smack*, they came together, *thump*, *crash*, bellowing, foaming, and drawing back to take a breath, and at it again, *smack! thump!* Ah ha! The bull has had enough! He is stunned. The old ox has him on the ground!

The ox catches up the bull on his horns. 'Peppi,' says he, 'tie the bull fast to my horns.'

Peppi did that, and they walked on, the ox carrying the bull on his horns.

When the bull came to himself, he said, 'Where am I?'

The ox said, 'You are on my horns.'

The bull said, 'Let me down; I am at your service.'

The ox said, 'When I have need of you, I will let you down.'

They walked, walked; they came to the king's city. There was a notice nailed up on the wall. The notice said, 'He who in one day can plough and harrow the king's barren field, shall marry the king's youngest daughter; or, if he prefers it, shall be given two tons of gold pieces. But he who tries and fails shall lose his head.'

'Peppi,' said the ox, 'we will plough and harrow that barren field. Go to the king.'

Peppi went to the king. 'Majesty, all hail!'

'Ragged boy, what do you want?'

'To plough and harrow your barren field in one day.'

'But, boy, have you read the notice carefully?'

'Majesty, I have. If I do not succeed, I lose my head. But I have nothing with me, because I am on my travels. Give me then a plough, a harrow, and a little hay for my oxen.'

The king said, 'You shall have those things. Bring your oxen into my stable. You can feed and water them there.'

Peppi brought the old ox and the bull into the king's stable. He untied the bull from the horns of the ox and said, 'Now, stand quiet.' The bull stood quiet. The old ox said, 'Peppi, to me half a sheaf of hay, to the bull a whole sheaf.'

Peppi gave them that, and went into the king's kitchen. The cook fed him well. They gave him a good bed, and he slept soundly.

In the morning, off he goes, with his ox and his bull, the plough and the harrow, some food for himself, and four sheaves of hay He comes to the barren field, and begins ploughing. Before mid-morning he had ploughed half the field, so he rested, ate a little food, and fed his beasts: to the old ox half a sheaf of hay, to the bull, a whole sheaf. Then he begins to plough again. My word he makes short work of it! And some of the king's counsellors are sitting on the palace balcony. They look towards the field and see what's doing. Then they hurry to the king.

'Your majesty, that scamp out there is doing what no man has done before! By noon he will have ploughed up the whole of the field; by sunset he will have harrowed it. Do you know what that means? You will have to give him your daughter.'

The king said, 'I don't want to give him my daughter. What do you advise?'

They said, 'Send him a roast chicken and a bottle of wine. Put a sleeping potion in the wine. That will fix him.'

So the king ordered up a roasted chicken and a bottle of wine with a sleeping potion in it. And at midday a servant girl carried chicken and wine to the field.

She said, 'Come, eat up, Peppi, before the meat gets cold.'

Peppi had now only a small corner of the field to plough. He unyoked the ox and the bull, fed them again: to the old ox a sheaf of hay, to the bull a sheaf and a half. Then he sat down to eat and drink. He eats all the chicken, he drinks all the wine. He falls asleep.

The old ox waits till the bull has finished his hay; then he goes to Peppi and kicks him, first with one hind foot, then with the other. *Blim, blam! Blim, blam!* 'Get up, get up, Peppi; your neck depends on it!'

Peppi rubs his eyes, gets up grumbling. The ox swings a pannikin of water into his face. 'Ah! Ah! You're right, my ox! You've saved my neck this time!' And he yokes up the beasts and sets to work. Well, he's not wasting any more time! He's soon finished the ploughing and begins harrowing.

The counsellors look from the balcony. They hurry to the king. 'That rascal is working quicker than any fiend! The sleeping potion in the wine was not strong enough – send him more and stronger!'

The servant girl brought the wine to Peppi. The sleeping potion in it was strong enough to put a body to sleep for a week. 'Come, drink to the king's health, Peppi!'

But Peppi says, 'No offence to his majesty, but his wine doesn't exactly suit my stomach.' And he tips it away on the earth and goes on harrowing. By sunset all is done. Peppi unyokes the ox and the bull, leads them back to the stable, gives them hay, and goes upstairs to the king.

'Good evening, your highness! Bless me, Papa!'

'Good evening, Peppi. So you have finished? What do you wish for now? Two tons of gold?'

'I am single, your majesty. What have I to do with gold? I want to get married.'

Well, no help for it! A bargain is a bargain. They give Peppi a bath in scented water, comb down his hair, dress him like a prince. He looks handsome now, and isn't he smiling! The king's youngest daughter smiles too when she sees him. 'Oh, what a pretty husband!'

So they are married.

Then Peppi went to show himself in all his finery to the ox, and the ox said, 'Peppi, I am going to die.'

'No, no, you shan't die, my ox!'

'Oh, yes, I shall. I am very, very old. Now listen to me. When I am dead, bury my hide and my flesh where you will, but keep my bones. One leg bone you must put under your pillow. The rest you must take out to the field you have ploughed and harrowed. And there you must plant them: the big bones spaced out in a pattern to cover all the field; the little bones set out in a pattern between them. You will do as I wish, Peppi?'

'I will do as you wish, my ox,' says Peppi. And there he is, blubbering.

So the ox lay down and died. And Peppi made a grave and buried the ox's hide and his flesh, and planted a rose bush over them. But the bones he kept in a basket, waiting for night.

And that night, when everyone was in bed, and Peppi's wife was asleep, Peppi slipped the ox's leg bone under the pillow. Then he took the basket with the rest of the bones out into the field. Peppi planted the bones as the ox had bidden him: the large ones spaced out in a pattern to cover all the field, the little ones spaced out in a pattern between them. He had just finished when the sun rose. And then he went back to bed.

By and by the princess, Peppi's wife, woke up laughing. 'Oh,' says she, 'what a dream I have had! I dreamed of cherries and apples and all manner of fruit. Such delicious fruit I was eating! And I dreamed of flowers, roses and pinks, jasmine and violets. Oh, what scent, what brightness and light! The scent of those flowers is still in my nostrils, and the taste of the fruit is still on my lips. . . . Why, Peppi, why, Peppi, the dream is true! See in my hand a bunch of cherries, and in your hand, Peppi, a bunch of grapes – oh, what beauties! And the scent of the flowers, Peppi, and the brightness and the light all about us!'

'Oh, my ox,' thought Peppi, 'this must be your doing!' But he said nothing.

All through the palace the brightness and light and the scent of

91

the flowers and the scent of the fruit was streaming. The king rose up and went out on to the balcony with his counsellors. They look towards the field which Peppi has ploughed and harrowed. What do they see? The field is full of trees, and the trees are full of all manner of fruit; and on the ground under the trees there are flowers and flowers and flowers, sparkling with dew and scenting the breeze that blows towards the palace.

The king orders out his carriage, he drives to the field. Can he believe his eyes? Yes, he must – oranges, lemons, apples, pears, plums, peaches, cherries, grapes, figs, apricots – there is no fruit tree you can name that isn't growing in that field, and all the trees laden down with fruit. The king plucks this fruit, plucks that fruit, he tastes, turns up his eyes, smacks his lips. He rejoices now that he gave Peppi to his daughter.

But how had Peppi managed it? That's what everyone wants to know. And none are more curious than the king's two other daughters, the elder sisters of Peppi's wife, who are both married to princes. They pester the princes, their husbands, to find out. But the princes say, 'How should we know? Go and ask Peppi's wife.'

So they go to Peppi's wife. 'Sister, how has your husband done all this?'

'I don't know.'

'Oh come, you must know!'

'On my life, I don't.'

'Well then, find out.' And they bother and bother till Peppi's wife says, 'Do stop it! I'll find out if I can.'

And that night when they went to bed, she said, 'Peppi, I have something to ask you.'

'Well then, ask away.'

'That field planted with fruit trees and flowers all in one night – how did you manage it?'

'I don't want to tell you.'

'Oh, Peppi, then you don't love me!'

'Yes, I love you, but I don't want to tell.'

But she bothered and wept, bothered and wept. She wouldn't let him sleep. So at last, for the sake of peace, he told her. And in the morning, she tells her sisters.

The sisters tell the two princes, their husbands. Ho, ho! The princes plot to get the better of Peppi. They go to him and say, 'Now, brother-in-law, Peppi, we must make a bet.'

Says Peppi, 'What about?'

Say they, 'We will bet all we possess, against all you possess, that by tomorrow morning we shall have found out how you made all those trees spring up in a single night, and what you made them of.'

'As you please,' says Peppi.

So they went to a notary and signed a deed. It seemed to Peppi very foolish. But it seemed worse than foolish next morning when the brothers-in-law came and said, 'Peppi, we have won the bet, thus and thus you did.' And they told everything and claimed all that Peppi possessed. So Peppi had to give them all his goods. Now he had nothing, not even his fine clothes. He had only his peasant's ragged blouse and tattered trousers and old boots. And dressed in these he went from the palace.

He went, went, went, he came to the hut of an old hermit with a beard down to his knees.

'Your blessing, little father.'

'You have my blessing, little son.'

'Can you tell me, little father, the way to where the sun rises?'

'No, I cannot. You must walk on till you come to the dwelling of one who is older and wiser than I am.'

So Peppi walked on, and came to the hut of an old hermit with a beard down to his feet.

'Your blessing, little father.'

'You have my blessing, little son. And what now?'

'Can you tell me, little father, the way to where the sun rises, that I may have speech with him?'

'Eh! Eh! That is beyond my knowing. But since you have come so far, take this sharp needle. Walk on. You will come to a lion who is crying aloud with pain. You will say to him. "Oh, comrade lion, your comrade hermit sends you greeting, and I bring this little needle to get the thorn out of your foot. And in return for the easing of your pain, I ask you to tell me how I may come to have speech with the sun".'

So Peppi walked on, and by and by he heard the lion crying aloud with pain, and came to where the lion stood on three feet and waving the other foot in the air. And Peppi said as the hermit had told him, and took the thorn out of the lion's foot with the sharp needle.

The lion said, 'Ah, you have saved my life!'

Peppi said, 'Then take me to where I may have speech with the sun.'

The lion said, 'Let us go.' And he led Peppi to a place where there was a great ocean of black water.

Then the lion said, 'You must stay here. Before the sun rises a winged serpent will look out of this black water. You must say "Oh, comrade serpent, your comrade lion sends you greeting, and bids you bring me to speech with the sun." '

Then the lion went off, and Peppi stood looking at the black water; and by and by it was rolling with waves, and a winged serpent put his head up out of the waves.

Peppi spoke to the serpent as the lion had told him, and the serpent said, 'Quick! Quick! Throw yourself into the water and creep under one of my wings, or when the sun appears his rays will set you on fire.'

So Peppi plunged into the black water, and hid under the serpent's wing. And the sun rose, turning the black water into flame.

Then the serpent lifted his wing out of the water, to make a shade before Peppi's eyes, and said, 'Peppi, say to the sun what you have to say, and say it quickly, before he goes on his way; for he waits for no man.'

And Peppi began to speak, 'Oh sun, traitor that you are! What have I done to you that you should betray me?'

'*I* betray you, Peppi?'

'Yes, you! Just as I had finished planting the barren field with my pattern of bones, you rose and saw me. And you, and you alone can have told my secret. Now I have lost my all, and what have you to say for yourself, oh, base and treacherous?'

The sun said, 'I did not betray you, Peppi; it was your wife. You told her your secret – and what could you expect?'

Then Peppi prayed the sun's forgiveness. And the sun said, 'I am grieved that you have lost your all. What can I now do to help you?'

Peppi said, 'You can do me a great favour. If tomorrow you set at nine o'clock in the evening instead of at eight, I can win back my goods from my brothers-in-law.'

'I will do you that favour, Peppi.'

Then the sun journeyed on, high into the sky. And Peppi went back to the palace.

He found his wife crying, very sorrowful that she had betrayed him. She brought him some soup. He rested and forgave her. Next morning his brothers-in-law came. 'What, Peppi, what! All in rags?' They mocked him.

Peppi said, 'Now, brothers-in-law, we must make another bet.'

The brothers-in-law said, 'Pooh! You have nothing more to wager.'

Peppi said, 'I will wager my neck. And you two must wager all your goods and the goods you took from me.'

'As you will, Peppi. But what shall we bet?'

'Tell me,' says Peppi, 'at what time does the sun set tonight?'

'Well, well, Peppi, every child knows that. The sun sets at eight o'clock.'

'Then we will bet,' says Peppi, 'that tonight the sun will not set till nine.'

'Peppi, are you crazy?'

'Crazy or no, that's the bet.'

'Done!'

So they went to a notary and signed a deed.

That evening they stood outside the palace to watch the sun. And the hour drew near to eight. What was the sun doing? Dropping quickly low, low into the west.

And when Peppi saw this, he cried out, 'Oh sun, is this the way you keep your promises?'

And the sun heard and remembered. Softly, slowly, oh, so slowly now, he wavered on his way. You might almost think he was standing still: but inch by inch he was going down. Inch by inch, with the clouds reddening above his head, for a full hour they saw him slowly, slowly sinking. Until as the clocks struck nine – behold he was gone!

'Didn't I say so?' said Peppi.

'You are right, Peppi,' said the brothers-in-law. 'Now we are beggars. All that we have, and all that we took from you, is yours.'

Peppi said, 'Your hearts are hardened by the ways of court. Now I will make you see the heart of a countryman. I don't want other people's things. You can keep all that belongs to you; I only want my own.'

The brothers-in-law said, 'You put us to shame, Peppi. We will do better from now on.'

And the king came and embraced Peppi. He took a circlet of gold and put it on Peppi's head. He made Peppi his heir. 'For,' said he, 'there is none worthier of a crown and a kingdom.'

So it came about that Peppi, from being a hungry oxherd, became a prince and heir to a throne.

12 · The Sun Mother

You must know that when the Storm King and the Sun King were both young, they lived in friendship. When the Sun King was tired out with a long day's work, the Storm King would call his people to water the earth. When the people prayed for rain, they got it. And when they prayed for sun, they got it. So those were happy days.

But one day when the Sun King met the Storm King, he found the Storm King in a raging temper. He was whirling round and stamping and flinging the clouds about.

'Why, brother, what's the matter?' said the Sun King.

'Don't dare to stop me!' shouted the Storm King. 'I'm off! I'm going to a land where there shall be so much rain that you'll never, never dry up that land again! Yes, I'll rain and rain and never stop raining for nine whole weeks!'

'But the people will suffer!' said the Sun King.

'Yes, and I *want* them to suffer!' shouted the Storm King.

'But why, brother, why?'

'Because the king of that land has a lovely daughter. I wanted her for my wife, but the king said, "No daughter for the Storm King." Now I'll show him – he and his people shall know who I am! I shall take all my servants – Rain and Wind, Thunder and Lightning, Hail and Snow – and let them all free to romp to their hearts' desire!'

'But, brother,' said the Sun King, 'the people in that land have done nothing to you! It would be very wrong to make them all suffer because the king has offended you.'

'I don't care. I *will* make them suffer! I *will!* I *WILL!*' shouted the Storm King. 'And who's to stop me?'

'I shall,' said the Sun King.

'I'd like to see you!' bawled the Storm King. And he hurried off.

But the Sun King, who had been on his way home, turned back. And if the Storm King hurried fast, the Sun King hurried faster. He got to that land before the Storm King. And when the Storm King drew near with all his servants to lay the land waste, the Sun King shone out so hotly, so brightly, that the Storm King's servants only just escaped being burned to death. So the Storm King, more furious now than ever, flew off with all his half-burned servants to his palace on the highest mountain in the world.

Next morning he set out with his servants to pester the land again. But again the Sun King was there before him, and again the Storm King had to retreat. So it went on for many days, until at last the Storm King was sitting in his mountain palace howling with rage to think that he was baulked of his revenge. And his servants, Rain and Wind, Thunder and Lightning, Hail and Snow, gathered round him to share his grief.

And then suddenly Wind gave a loud hoot. '*Hoo! Hoo! Hoo!* Master,' said he, 'I have a plan! You know that when the Sun King flies out each morning he is but a little child. By midday he has grown into a strong man. But in the evening he comes home a tired, grey-haired old totterer to sleep in his mother's lap. Should he not sleep in his mother's lap he would remain a feeble old man. Well, then, we must take the Sun Mother prisoner.'

Then all the Storm King's servants began to rejoice and shriek.

'*Knarr! Klirrr!*' screamed Snow and Hail. 'A splendid plan!'

'*Bumbara, Bumbara! Bumbara, Bu-mmm!*' roared Thunder. 'Three cheers for Wind!' Whilst Lightning ran continually from one corner of the palace to the other, shrieking, '*Zickzack! Zickzack!* That's what we'll do!'

99

And Rain was whispering, '*Tritsch! Tratsch! Tritsch! Tratsch!* Oh Wind, I love you like a brother!'

'Silence!' commanded the Storm King. 'I have to think. It may be a good plan, but the Sun Mother is not to be caught by shouting. . . . Ah, I have it!'

So what did the Storm King do? He turned himself into a winged grey horse; and at a time when the Sun King was far from home he flew off to the Sun Mother's house.

The Sun Mother was sitting before the door of her golden house. The winged grey horse alighted at her feet.

'Good morrow, Sun Mother!'

'Good morrow, grey horse.'

'Sun Mother, I am the Wind Horse. I bring a message from the Sun King. He begs you to come quickly. He is in a flooded land; he has used up all his strength, and yet he cannot dry it. He would sleep for an hour in your lap that he may get new strength.'

'Wind Horse, this is very strange! Never before has my son sent me such a message. But yes, I must go to him. Take me on your back that we may hurry!'

So the Sun Mother gets on to the grey horse. The grey horse spreads his wings. Off they rush through the air, fast, fast, faster. He brings the Sun Mother to the entrance of an underground cave. He turns back into the Storm King. He pushes the Sun Mother down into the cave, piles earth over the opening, stamps the earth down with all his might, and rushes off in a gale of laughter.

In the evening the Sun King came back to his mother's golden house. What is he now? A grey-haired weary old man. 'Sun Mother, take me in your lap that I may sleep and grow young again! Sun Mother! Sun Mother!' he calls in his weary old voice. No one answers. He creeps into the golden house. 'Sun Mother! Sun Mother!' No one is there. He sinks to sleep on the golden floor. And in the morning when he wakes he is still a grey-haired weary old man. He has no strength to fly out and brighten the earth.

Now over all the earth there is a great darkness.

And in that darkness the Storm King and his servants play havoc. Lightning flashes, Thunder roars, Wind howls, Rain falls in torrents. Hail bombards the cowering earth. Snow covers it with an icy blanket. The Storm King rushes from end to end of the earth, shouting his triumph. Ah, the poor people, the poor people – how can they live under such a terror?

But down in her dark cavern the Sun Mother is watching her

fingers. The nails on her fingers are growing, long, long, longer; and as they grow she sharpens them on a stone. And when they are long and sharp as little knives, she digs with them through the earth that blocks the entrance to the cavern: digs, digs, till she has made a hole, creeps through the hole, and hurries back to her golden house.

In that golden house the Sun King, a grey-haired tired old man, lies where he has fallen, awake but too weak to move. The Sun Mother sits and takes his head in her lap. She weeps over him, she croons over him, she sings him to sleep. All night long he sleeps with his head in her lap. And when he wakes in the morning – what is he? A bright-haired smiling child.

The bright-haired smiling child flies off to circle the earth. And as he flies he becomes ever stronger and stronger, bigger and bigger, and the light that blazes about his shining head grows ever more brilliant. Before that shining, Lightning and Thunder flee, Wind shudders and is silent, Rain, Hail and Snow creep away, the Storm King rushes howling to his mountain palace, and all his servants follow him.

Then the happy earth clothed herself in fresh green, the happy trees put forth new leaves, the happy birds sang among the branches, the happy beasts ran and leaped; and the happy, happy people laughed and whistled as they went about their work.

And after that day the Sun Mother was never again tricked into leaving her golden house. When the tired old Sun King came home to that golden house in the evening, he always found the Sun Mother waiting to lull him to sleep in her lap, and to send him forth, strong and young in the morning.

But alas, the Sun King and the Storm King were never friends again.

13 · The White Lamb

Well now, there's a sea captain, and there's his lovely little daughter, Rosalie, and there's the fairy godmother who came to Rosalie's christening and set a little red mark, like a strawberry, on her left ear; and there's a stepmother, whom the captain married after his first wife died, so that there should be someone to take care of his little daughter, Rosalie, whilst he was away at sea. And the step-mother has a little girl called Gemma, who is not beautiful like Rosalie, though she has a good honest face. So there you are: sea captain, Rosalie, fairy godmother, stepmother and Gemma, five people. And here's the story of what happened to them.

The two children, Rosalie and Gemma, loved each other dearly – they were both jewels of little girls, that they were! But the step-mother was a bad wicked woman, and she hated Rosalie for being more beautiful than her own child. Well, the stepmother had a flock of sheep, and one morning, when the captain was away at sea, she sent Rosalie out into the fields to mind the sheep. She didn't give Rosalie any breakfast, either: she thrust a great bundle of flax and a spindle into the child's hands and said, 'I won't have you idling your time away out in the fields! You must spin all this flax before you come home. And if it isn't spun to my liking, you won't get any supper.'

Rosalie didn't know how to spin. She drove the sheep out into the fields and sat down on the grass and cried. And there came to her a beautiful lady, carrying a covered basket. And the lady said, 'Little one, why are you crying?'

'I'm crying because I'm hungry,' said Rosalie. 'And because my stepmother says I must spin all this flax, and I don't know how to spin. And please, who are you?'

'I am your fairy godmother,' said the lovely lady. 'And here in this basket you will find food and drink. Don't bother about the spinning, I will come again at sunset.' And when she had said that, the lovely lady took the flax and the spindle and disappeared.

Rosalie opened the basket. It was full of the most delicious food, and there was a big flask of milk as well. Rosalie ate and drank, and when she could eat no more, there was still enough food left in the basket for her dinner. So she ran about the fields all day, and picked the flowers, and sang little songs, and played with the sheep. And at sunset her godmother came again, bringing the flax all beautifully spun. It was a happy Rosalie who drove the sheep home that evening.

But was the stepmother pleased when Rosalie gave her the spun flax? Oh, dear me, no, she wasn't! She was so angry that she wouldn't give Rosalie any supper. She gave her a beating instead. Rosalie went to bed crying; and Gemma went to bed crying too, because she couldn't bear to see Rosalie beaten. So the two children sobbed themselves to sleep in each other's arms.

Every day after that the stepmother sent Rosalie out into the fields to mind the sheep, and gave her only a crust of bread for breakfast, and a good beating to go with it. And every day the horrid woman gave Rosalie some impossible task which must be done before she came home: a whole lot of stockings to knit out of a bundle of tangled wool, or six petticoats to embroider before sunset, or some odd scraps of linen to make into a dress. But every day the fairy godmother came with a basket of food, and took away the tangled wool, or the six petticoats, or the scraps of linen, and came again at sunset with the stockings knitted, or the petticoats embroidered, or the dress made. And if Rosalie's back was bruised and aching from the stepmother's beatings, the fairy godmother had but to stroke the back with her gentle fingers, and the bruises vanished and the ache was healed.

So instead of little Rosalie growing thin and weak and ugly as the stepmother hoped, she grew every day stronger and more beautiful. Her cheeks were rosy, her eyes sparkled; and as for the little strawberry mark on her left ear – well, nobody would have noticed that, for her shining hair fell over her ears and covered it.

The stepmother went about the house stamping and muttering. 'I can't understand it,' she said. 'Someone must be feeding that child! Tomorrow, Gemma, you must follow Rosalie to the fields, and hide behind the hedge and watch.'

'Oh no, no, no, Mother!' cried Gemma.

'Oh yes, yes, yes!' snapped the stepmother. 'Will you do as I tell you, or must I beat you also?'

'I will do as you tell me, Mother,' said Gemma meekly.

So next day, after Rosalie had driven the sheep to the fields, Gemma followed and went behind the hedge and hid. By and by she heard Rosalie laughing. So she peeped over the hedge. What did she see? She saw Rosalie sitting on the grass with a basket on her knees. She was taking food out of the basket and eating. And every now and then she looked up and laughed. She was talking to someone, too – but there was no one there! Gemma felt frightened. She crept away from behind the hedge and ran home.

'Well,' said the stepmother, 'what did you see?'

'I – I saw no one but Rosalie,' said Gemma. 'No one at all.'

'Then tomorrow I shall go myself,' said the stepmother.

And go she did, and hid behind the hedge, and peeped over it, and saw Rosalie with the basket on her knees. But nothing else did she see. So then the stepmother jumped from behind the hedge and ran to Rosalie screaming, 'What have you got in that basket?' And she snatched the basket and turned it upside down.

What fell out? Flowers, flowers, and more flowers.

'I'll teach you to waste your time picking flowers!' screamed the

stepmother. And she boxed Rosalie's ears, and trampled the flowers under her heel, and ran home again, muttering with rage because she had found out nothing.

Then the fairy godmother, who was standing all the time at Rosalie's side, said, 'Little goddaughter, you won't see me again for a long time. I have to go on a journey to the land of my people, for we are choosing a new queen to rule over us, and all we fairies are ordered home to cast our votes and attend the coronation. But here is something that will keep you safe and happy whilst I am away.' And she gave Rosalie a charm in the shape of a tiny gold wand. 'You have but to touch the wand and wish, and it will give you anything you ask for. But take heed, take heed, my darling, that your stepmother doesn't steal the wand from you. For she wishes you ill, and desires nothing but your death.'

Then, having given her the charm, the fairy kissed Rosalie on the forehead and vanished.

That evening Rosalie stitched up a little bag, put the fairy's charm into it, and pinned the bag inside the bodice of her dress. Now indeed she was safe and happy. She had but to touch the wand and ask for food, and she got food, as much as she could eat. And when the stepmother beat her, she had but to put her hand against the place where the wand was hidden, and the blows might have been snowflakes, so softly and harmlessly did they fall.

But what about the sea captain, Rosalie's father, you may be asking, for he seems to have dropped right out of the story. Well, he'll be coming in again by and by. But he's gone on a long voyage right to the other side of the world, and he's having enough adventures of his own, what with savages and storms, to keep any man busy. Meantime the days passed, and the years passed, and Rosalie grew from a lovely child into a beautiful young girl and the village lads came hanging around, trying to coax a word or a smile out of her. The village lads didn't take much notice of Gemma. Was Gemma jealous? Not she! She loved Rosalie too much to wish her anything but good. But the stepmother was jealous enough for the two of them.

'I must get rid of that girl,' thought the stepmother. 'And I *will* get rid of that girl!' And off she stamped to consult a witch she knew of.

The witch said, 'Rosalie has a little magic wand to protect her. The wand is sewn up in a bag pinned inside her bodice. Bring me the wand, and I'll see what I can do.'

'But how to get it?' said the stepmother.

'That's your affair,' said the witch.

So what did the stepmother do? Next morning she told Gemma that she must go on an errand to the village. And before Gemma set off, she gave her a cup of warm milk. And no sooner was Gemma out of the house than the stepmother scowled at Rosalie and said, 'Well, I suppose you must have a cup of milk too; or when your father comes home you'll tell him I starve you!' And she handed Rosalie a cup of milk.

Well, Rosalie, glad enough to think that her stepmother was being kind for once, drank off the milk. What happened? Her head nodded, her eyes closed; she sank down on the settle fast asleep, for that cup of milk was drugged.

Then the stepmother undid Rosalie's bodice, unpinned the little bag in which the charm was hidden, and carried bag and wand off to the witch.

'Ho!' says the witch. 'What do you want now?'

'I want Rosalie changed into a black sheep,' says the stepmother.

'I can't do that,' says the witch. 'The girl's much too good. Nobody can make white black. All I *can* do is to change her into a white lamb.'

'Well, do that, and be quick about it!' says the stepmother.

So the witch muttered some spells and stirred something in a cauldron. 'There, that's done,' says she. 'You can go back home now. Here, take this charm with you. *I* don't want it! But see you keep it safe from prying eyes and thieving fingers.'

So the stepmother took the charm and hurried away. When she got home – what did she see? A little white lamb, with a strawberry mark on its left ear, shivering in a corner of the kitchen.

The stepmother gave a screech of laughter. She picked up the lamb, tucked it under her arm, and stamped off with it, up hill and down dale, till she came to the overgrown garden of a ruined castle. And there she dumped it down.

'And if it wasn't for the kindness of my heart,' said she, 'I'd have drowned you in the nearest pond!' And so off home with her again, and screeching with laughter.

What did she do next? She bought a coffin, filled it full of stones, and hammered down the lid. She dabbled her face in a bowl of water, to make out she was shedding tears. And when Gemma came back from her errand, that's what she saw – a nailed-down coffin, and the stepmother sitting by it all slobbered up with make believe tears.

'Rosalie is dead!' howled the stepmother. 'And what the captain will say when he comes home, I don't like to think!'

'I don't, I can't, I won't believe it!' cried Gemma. But she wept all the same, and *her* tears were real ones.

The stepmother had the coffin that was full of stones buried in the churchyard. She rigged up herself and Gemma in black clothes, and made a great show of mourning. But the evil glee inside her kept bubbling up and making her laugh. She threw Rosalie's charm into the fire; but the charm wouldn't burn. So she took up a piece of board from under the kitchen dresser, dug a hole in the ground where the board had been, put the charm into the hole, covered it with earth, and replaced the board. 'And there you can lie till doomsday!' said she.

Well, after a while the captain comes home from the sea – a sad homecoming for him! He mourned for his little daughter and wouldn't be comforted. He had no heart to go to sea again. He dismissed his crew, sold his ship, and took to wandering about the countryside like one who had lost his wits. 'Oh, my Rosalie, my little Rosalie!' he moaned. 'Light of my life, joy of my heart! I shall never, never see you again!'

And in the deserted garden of the ruined castle the little white lamb nibbled the rank grass and ran about bleating, 'Oh, my father, my dear, dear father! Your little daughter is here! Come to me, Father, come, come, come!'

And one day, as the captain wandered about like one who has lost his wits, it so happened that he strayed near to the ruined castle, and heard that pitiful bleating. And he climbed over a broken wall into the castle garden. What did he see? A white lamb who ran to him, '*Baa! Baa! Baa!*' and rubbed its little head against his knee.

The captain stooped and fondled the lamb. 'Ah, how sweetly pretty you are, my little creature! You have eyes like my Rosalie, mild and good. And you have on your little ear a strawberry mark just like hers! Come, I will take you home with me, little sweet one; you shan't live lonely here!'

But the lamb kicked up its little heels and ran away. Nothing the captain could do would persuade it to go home with him.

Next day the captain went to visit the lamb again; and this time he took Gemma with him. '*Baa! Baa! Baa!*' the lamb ran to greet them both; it wagged its little tail, it leaped up and nuzzled Gemma's face. And Gemma sat down and took the lamb in her lap, and wept – though why she wept she couldn't have said.

Every day the captain and Gemma went to visit the lamb; they took it bread and cake and sweet corn. The stepmother became suspicious; she wanted to know where they went and why; and the captain – the innocent man that he was! – told her. So then the stepmother scowled and said to herself, 'I must see into this!' And next morning, when the captain and Gemma set off to visit the lamb, there was the stepmother stamping along beside them.

So they came to the castle garden. But as soon as the lamb saw the stepmother it fled away and hid: nor, though they searched and called, searched and called, could they find where it was hidden.

That lamb remained hidden. Day after day the captain went to the garden to look for it, but never could he find it. He called, called, and sometimes he thought he heard a faint bleating, like the tiniest whisper, from somewhere among the ruins. But when he went to search those ruins, he found nothing there.

And one day, as he was wandering about the castle gardens and calling, he saw a beautiful lady coming towards him. And the lady said, 'What do you seek?'

'I am searching for a little lamb, my lady. I have bread and cake for it in this basket. If it belongs to you, I pray you tell me where it is hidden.'

'Belongs to me?' said the beautiful lady. 'Nay, captain, it belongs to you! Haven't you recognized the strawberry mark on its ear? Sit down by me, for I have much to tell you.'

So the captain sat down on a pile of ruins, and the beautiful lady sat beside him, and told him all about the wickedness of the stepmother, and about the witch, and the stealing of the charm, and the turning of Rosalie into a white lamb. And when she had finished her story, the lamb came from behind the pile of ruins and rubbed against them, baaing and wagging its tail. And the captain took the lamb in his arms.

'I will not go back to that wicked woman!' said he. 'I will come and live with you, little lamb, amongst these ruins.'

'You will do no such thing!' said the beautiful lady, who, as you will have guessed, was Rosalie's fairy godmother just returned from her long journey. 'You will go home at once, and you will hurry. You must find and bring back the charm that I gave my goddaughter, and which the stepmother has buried under the kitchen dresser. With that charm I can free Rosalie – but hasten, hasten! For even now the witch has got wind of my return; she has flown to tell the stepmother, and the stepmother is about to dig up the charm. And once she holds it in her hand, even I am powerless against her, so potent is that charm!'

The captain did hasten. He ran, ran. When he got home, the house door was open, and from inside came sounds of bumping and thumping, as if something heavy was being moved about. Quietly, quietly, the captain tiptoed into the kitchen. What did he see? The dresser dragged out from the wall, a floorboard moved from under it, and the witch and the stepmother on their knees, scooping up earth in handfuls. And aren't they scolding!

'You needn't have buried it so deep!' snarls the witch.

'Hold your tongue!' snaps the stepmother. 'I'll have it up in a minute!'

But the captain leaps upon them: a blow with his right fist, a blow with his left fist; the witch and the stepmother, taken by surprise, topple over, cracking their heads, one against the wall, the other against the dresser. The captain is on his knees, tossing the earth out of the hole they have dug. Ah, he has found the little bag now! He leaps up, holding it tight in his hand. The stepmother may shout and curse, the witch may shriek out one spell after another: the captain, holding the charm, is unmoved alike by spells and curses.

So he left them to their rages, and hastened back to the ruined garden, where the fairy was waiting for him, holding the lamb in her arms.

'Take the wand out of the bag and lay it on the ground,' said the fairy.

The captain did that, and the fairy put down the lamb. 'Now, my little one,' said she, 'touch the wand with your feet.'

The lamb set one forefoot on the wand. It gave a skip and set the other forefoot on the wand. It gave two more skips and set its hind feet on the wand. And then it gave such a skip that it leaped right into the air and came down head over heels. '*Ba-a-a-a!* . . . *Ha-a-a-a!*' No lamb now, but lovely laughing Rosalie, running to hug and kiss her father.

So, after they had kissed and rejoiced together, they came out of the ruined garden, and set off for home, and the fairy went with them. And when they got near home, there was Gemma coming to meet them. And it was 'darling, darling Rosalie!' And 'darling, darling Gemma!' and the two girls laughing and hugging each other and crying for joy.

But what about the witch and the stepmother? Well, the witch had flown off on her broomstick; she wasn't going to have anything more to do with any of them, and so she had told the stepmother. But the stepmother was nowhere to be seen. Gemma knew where she was, but Gemma wouldn't tell. After all, however wicked the woman was, she was still Gemma's mother.

'Ask the wand,' said the fairy.

So the captain asked the wand, and the wand said, 'Up the chimney.' Then the captain looked up the chimney and called, 'Come down, you wicked woman! You and I have a score to settle!'

And a shrieking voice answered him from up the chimney. 'I am not coming down. I shall never come down, never, never, never!' And each time the voice said 'Never' it grew shriller and shriller, until at last it was a mere squeak. And then something flew out from the top of the chimney. And that something was a big, black bat. And whether it was the fairy or the witch who had turned the stepmother into a bat, I can't tell you; but a bat she was, and a bat she remained. The bat flew away and hung herself upside down on the branch of a great tree, and never came near the captain's house again.

So the captain and Rosalie and Gemma lived in happiness. And by and by, when the girls were quite grown up, the fairy godmother saw to it that they both got handsome husbands.

14 · Rubizal

The demon Rubizal lived in the mountains, and the mountains belonged to him, as everybody knew except a few clever people who said that such things as demons didn't exist. And among these clever ones was a rich lord of the manor, whose lands lay at the foot of the mountains.

Now one day this lord of the manor went walking in the mountains with some of his boon companions. And as they were so walking, they talked of Rubizal.

'He is very powerful,' said one.

'And he can be very kind,' said another.

'But we should do ill to vex him,' said a third. 'For then he can be terrible!'

The lord of the manor laughed long and loud. 'Fools! Fools!' cried he. 'Can you really believe such nonsense?'

And he began to bawl out, 'Hey, Rubizal! Hey, Rubizal! Come and show yourself, old humbug! Here are some disciples of yours waiting to kiss your hands!'

'Oh, hush, hush!' cried his companions.

But the lord of the manor wouldn't hush. He bawled louder and louder, calling Rubizal all sorts of rude names.

And of course Rubizal heard. But he didn't show himself. 'All in good time!' thought he.

Well, the lord of the manor, having bawled himself hoarse, felt thirsty and hungry too. And now he was complaining about the heat, and blaming his companions for not having brought anything to eat with them, and of there being nothing to drink but spring water, when not far ahead of them appeared a most magnificent tavern, the like of which you wouldn't find in all the country round.

One of the companions, who had been that way before, and had seen no such tavern, was scared, and said, 'Pray heaven something isn't coming adrift now!' But the lord of the manor gave a shout of laughter and said, 'Hey, boys, it's already come adrift!' And he pulled a piece of leather from the sole of his boot, which he had torn against a rock. So they all laughed, and came to the tavern.

They were received by servants in splendid uniforms, who showed them into a fine large dining room; and the magnificence of that room, could you but see it, would leave you gasping. The walls were hung with pictured tapestry: there were snowy mountains in the pictures, and green glens, glittering water springs and cool dark forests with birds among the branches, and all manner of animals sauntering through the forest glades. And over all rose a domed and painted ceiling, with white clouds sailing across a blue sky, and a new-risen sun brightening the edges of the clouds.

Oh and oh! the lord's companions were staring and exclaiming; but the lord himself was loudly demanding to be served. Then came the host, a tall, handsome man, bowing and smiling. The table was soon spread with everything of the best, and the lord and his companions sat down to the most delicious meal they had ever tasted. And though the lord of the manor must be talking big, and bragging and boasting of his own table, and of how much better he was used to being served, his companions did nothing but gobble and laugh. And as dish followed dish, and bottle followed bottle, even the lord himself was at last joining in the merriment.

But all at once the room, the table, the waiters, and the host himself, began to take on strange appearances: in the tapestries

the birds began to sing and hop, the waterfalls to rush and roar, the trees to sway, the wild swine to scamper and grunt, the cattle to bellow, the dogs to rush barking through the forest glens chasing the fleeing deer; and under the trees in the cool dark forest, wolves and lions stalked and roared.

And the waiters – what were they? One was a withered tree stump, one a piece of rock, one a stork, another a cockchafer, another a wasp. As to the host himself, he was making the strangest faces: now he grinned, now he wept, now he had one eye, now he had three eyes, now he had a hundred eyes; now he shrunk to the size of a dwarf, now he reared up to the size of a giant; now he had a small swollen nose, now a nose like a beak, now he had a human face, now a goat's face, now a pig's face; now he spoke like a man, now he bleated like a sheep, now he grunted like a wild pig, now he roared like a lion. And what's more, the clouds on the ceiling began to move, a rushing wind drove them apart, then drove them together again. Lightning flashed among the clouds, thunder rolled; then the sky cleared for a moment, stars glittered in its dark depths; a full moon rose and dimmed the stars. . . .

But the room, what was happening to the room? The trees and the cliffs were growing higher and higher; the trees closed in, the rocks drew closer together, and parted, and drew still closer. The terrified lord of the manor and his terrified companions crept shuddering under the table: but the table rose and vanished, and there they were, crouched among the threatening cliffs, that grew closer and closer and closer together.

'Sir host, sir host!' cried the terrified lord of the manor, 'Am I dreaming or waking? Truly one could almost believe this to be the doing of a mountain spirit, if that wasn't such a manifest absurdity! Sir host, tell me, what does it mean?'

The host didn't answer. He was making madder faces than ever. And now the sky on the ceiling was black with clouds, rain fell in torrents: now everything was lit by a flash of lightning, now thunder pealed and everything was dark. . . .

'Sir host, sir host,' faltered the lord of the manor. 'What is your opinion? Might this perhaps be the work of a mountain spirit whom men call Rubizal?'

Hardly had the lord spoken that word *Rubizal*, when there came such a clap of thunder that the whole room shuddered. Every beast on the tapestried walls raised his voice in an ear-splitting cater-wauling; the trees bent and shuddered under the howling gale; the rocks split and rolled this way and that; the very mountains shuddered; and ever more violently fell the rain, and ever more swiftly one flash of lightning followed another, and ever more loudly came the clap and the rumbling of the thunder. And then suddenly the whole ceiling of the room rose into the air, higher and higher, till it vanished among the clouds, the room and everything in it disappeared, and the lord and his companions found themselves seated on the ground among the familiar mountains.

All drew a breath of relief. The lord of the manor gave a foolish laugh. 'We must have fallen asleep,' said he. 'I have had a strange and terrifying dream; but now let us go home.' He got to his feet . . . 'My head feels strangely heavy,' said he, and he put up his hand to his head.

Oh me! What did he find? Two long hairy grey ears adorned his lordly head. And his companions – oh me, his companions! One had antlers on his head, another had a pig's snout, another a dog's muzzle, another a duck's beak, another a weasel's face, another the head of a toad – all, all wore some hideous disguise.

For a moment they stood silent and appalled; then with one voice they began to blame the lord of the manor whose unbelief had brought them into this calamity . . . With one voice, did I say? No, with a dozen voices: the hiss of a serpent, the howl of a dog, the squeal of a pig, the quack of a duck, the bellowing of a bull – for one moment all was uproar. And then, squealing, howling, bellowing, and hissing, they fell upon the lord of the manor, who turned and fled.

Now began such a chase as the world had never seen before. All night long they pursued the fleeing long-eared one among the mountains; until at dawn both pursued and pursuers dropped exhausted to the ground and fell into a deep sleep.

When they woke they were lying by a waterfall high, high up in the mountains, the sun was shining, and far off they heard the singing of birds. Their disguises had dropped from them; they were themselves once more. So they went in silence down the mountain, feeling too shattered to speak. Only when they found themselves once more amongst houses and people did their courage return to them.

'We must never, never speak of this!' said the lord of the manor.

'No, never, never,' they all agreed.

But, there you are, the lord of the manor was soon again airing his views about the foolishness of believing in demons and such like. And his companions, who had now little respect for him, were soon whispering slyly in his ear: 'What was it then that you were wearing on your head the other day? And what about pigs' snouts, and ducks' beaks? And did we dream of a tavern on the mountains, and of tapestries that came alive, and of ceilings that poured down rain?'

So one way and another, the story got about. And it was told to me, and now I have told it to you.

15 · Tredrill

Janey Tregeer's baby was the sweetest little thing ever you set eyes on. 'Pretty as a peach,' the neighbours said, and so it was. Well, one sunny morning, Janey wrapped her sleeping baby in a shawl, and off with her to work in the hayfield, carrying the baby with her. She laid it down under the hedge, and worked for an hour or two. When the baby woke and cried she ran to feed it. After that she hushed the baby to sleep again, and then went on working. So between working and tending the baby, Janey's day passed, and it came sunset. Then Janey put down her rake, straightened her tired back, picked up the baby and went home.

By this time it was dusky in her little kitchen. Janey laid the baby down in its cradle, and lit a candle. Then she stooped over the cradle again. The dear of him, the dear of him, how lovesome he always looked when sleeping! . . . But what's this? Tonight he doesn't look lovesome at all: his little face has gone all wrinkled like a little old man's, and when he opens his eyes, those eyes aren't blue as they should be – they're a horrid bright glaring green!

Janey gives such a scream that all the neighbours rush in. And when she cries out, 'Oh, oh, the fairies have stolen my baby and put this thing in its place!' – well, the neighbours agree that the thing in the cradle isn't Janey's baby. There they are, all talking together, and the little thing glaring up at them with its green eyes, when in comes Janey's husband from bedding down the squire's horses.

'What's to do here?' says he, none too pleased. But when he saw the thing in the cradle, the poor man sat down and covered his face with his hands. 'I wouldn't have had it happen, no I wouldn't have had it happen, not for a five pound note!' says he.

Next morning Janey got up early and trudged over moor to consult a wise woman. And the wise woman said, 'It's a changeling you've got there, my dear, and the only thing to do with it is to carry it every Wednesday at dawn of day up to Chapel Well. There, just as the sun comes up, you must dip the creature into the well, and then carry it widdershins, that is the opposite way to the way the sun's going, three times round the well. Maybe the charm will work, maybe it won't. But I know of naught else that will.'

So every Wednesday there was Janey rising before dawn, and trudging with the creature on her back (for it wouldn't lie quiet in her arms) the mile or more up from her cottage to Chapel Well. And when she dipped it into the cold, cold water, that imp screamed with laughter; and when she passed it widdershins three times round the well, it was giggling and chuckling to itself in a manner more like a foolish old man than a baby. And all the way home it would still be giggling.

And then how it ate! There was no satisfying its appetite, and yet it didn't grow any bigger; and however much it was stuffed with food, it remained thin as a stick.

Poor Janey was beside herself with the plague it was to her. And as to Janey's husband – if he didn't run off and leave her, he came nigh to doing it many a time. There was no peace at all in that little house. Janey was most of her time in tears, and quarrelling with her man, and he with her, both of them on edge because of the thing in the cradle. But they had neither of them the heart to do it any harm.

Well now, one Wednesday in May, Janey takes the thing on her back, and sets out in a pour of rain to carry it up to Chapel Well. And in a lonely place, very near to the top of the hill, she hears

the strangest voice. The voice is coming up from the ground. And this is what it's saying:

'Tredrill, Tredrill, thy wife and children greet thee well.'

Oh me, oh me, that was bad enough – that a voice should be speaking where nobody was; but worse, far worse it was when the thing on her back sang out in a little squeaky voice:

'For wife and child
Nothing care I,
They may laugh,
Or they may cry –
Whilst milk I quaff
When I am dry,

122

Get of pap my fill
Whenever I will,
And on the dowdy's back I ride
With my little legs astride,
When we go up to work the spell
And play the fool at Chapel Well.'

Oh, it was all too much! Janey shook the thing off her back, and dumped it down on the ground. 'Go back to thy wife and child, varmint!' she screamed, and ran back home as if Old Scritch was after her. But bless me, when she got home, there was the creature lying in the cradle and grinning at her!

No, it was very clear, the wise woman's charm hadn't worked. Then what to do now? The neighbours came in and all began talking together as usual. One said one thing, one said another. But the oldest of them – and she was Janey's great-grandma – said, 'I seem to remember me of a thing the like of this happening once afore. And what the people did then was to carry the creature into the churchyard, lay it under the stones of the stile, and leave it there until midnight.'

Well, that was a new idea, and they all agreed there was no harm in trying. So off with the whole lot of them to the church-yard, with the creature up on Janey's back, and giggling to itself. When they came to the churchyard stile, Janey laid the creature down under the stones of the stile. She wrapped it in an old shawl too, because, though she couldn't bear the sight of the ugly little thing, still she was tender-hearted, and she didn't want it to take cold, with night coming on and all.

And when that shawl was put round it, the creature stopped giggling, and gave a proper smile.

'Now we must all go away and leave it be,' says Janey's great-grandma. So the other women went home. But Janey wouldn't go home; she kept running about round the church – she was that anxious she couldn't keep still. And the great-grandma stayed with her, lest she go poking back under the stile and break the spell; for that's what Janey was making to do, more than once.

'Isn't it midnight, isn't it midnight *yet*?' she kept crying.

'No, t'aint,' says great-grandma, catching hold of her.

But at last it *was* midnight, and they both hurried to the stile. What did they see by the light of the stars – oh, what did they see? Janey's own beautiful baby, sound asleep under the stones of the stile, and wrapped in a handsome silk shawl, embroidered with silver flowers.

'My baby! My baby!' Janey picked it up and covered its soft little face with kisses. Then, with the great-grandma trotting along beside her, Janey carried her baby home. And as they went they heard all round them in the night shrill peals of fairy laughter.